I0542429

TIME GAP

What happens when past and present collide?

NIKKI BROADWELL

Airmid Publishing

Tucson, Arizona

Time Gap

Copyright © 2016 Nikki Broadwell
All rights reserved

This is a work of fiction. All names, places and ideas presented here, with
the exception of a few historical names, are products of the author's
imagination. Any resemblance to anyone living or dead is purely
coincidental.

Cover by Valerie Howard
Formatting by Perry Elizabeth Design

ISBN-10: 0-9979941-4-2
ISBN-13: 978-0-9979941-4-8

Airmid Publishing
www.nikkibroadwell.com

Other books by Nikki:

Wolfmoon series:
Moonstone
Willow
Raven
Faery

Gypsy Series:
Gypsy's Quest
Gypsy's Return
Gypsy's Secret

Just Another Desert sunset
Coyote Sunrise

Summer McCloud paranormal mystery series:
Murder in Plain Sight
Saffron and Seaweed
Black and White and *Red* all Over

The Bridge

A Witch in Time Saves Nine

https://www.amazon.com/Nikki-Broadwell/e/B007EE1LN0

"People like us, who believe in physics, know that the distinction between past, present, and future is only a stubbornly persistent illusion."

~Albert Einstein

PROLOGUE

I reached out in the dark to touch the damp walls of stone that formed my prison. The tiny cell closed in, sending terror clawing up my throat. Was there any air in here? Because I was gasping now, trying to breathe. I screamed and kept on screaming, choking and wheezing as I used up even more air, but I knew no one could hear me through the foot thick walls. As my throat closed, my belly clutched. I hugged my knees close trying to control my panic. It was no use. My claustrophobia had taken over and no amount of telling myself there was air could stop the feeling of suffocating. If they didn't come soon I was sure I would die here.

CHAPTER ONE

AIRY

"You must stop seeing this boy, Airy! Are you having sex? Are you on birth control?"

I glared at my mother, noticing that her green eyes had darkened, as though a shadow had come over them. Had she really traveled all the way from Otherworld just to scold me? "For one thing his name is Fehin, and for another I'm eighteen. You can no longer order me around as though I'm a child! Where's Dad?" I asked, looking around for the one person who stood up for me in these sorts of dealings. "Does he agree?"

Her lips pressed together. "Your father and I are of like mind, Airy. He doesn't want this going on any more than I do."

"Why? What's so bad about Fehin? I don't understand."

"You would if—"

"If what? Just tell me what's going on!" I shouted. I looked around the little park, glad to see no one within hearing distance. The sun had gone behind clouds, casting a chill across my bare arms despite it being August.

My mother sighed and ran nervous fingers through her tangle of red hair the same color as mine. Last year I'd gone through a similar argument with both her and my grandparents regarding Fehin. No one had ever explained the extreme need to break us up. I'd finally concluded that they just didn't want me hooked up with anyone, especially a boy who had been on drugs and nearly died because of it. But Fehin was special and magical, and his life here in the twenty-first century had weakened him, that and his horrible half brother, Wolf. Wolf had pushed the drugs on him when Fehin was vulnerable. But Fehin managed to pull himself out of the darkness. Why couldn't my mother see him for who he was now?

I shuddered, my mind going to the root cellar where Wolf had left me to die. If Fehin hadn't found me I wouldn't be here now. I'd explained this to my mother over and over, but she didn't seem to care. "Well? Do you have any explanation? I can't imagine anything that would stop us, though. We love each other, or hadn't you considered that?"

My mother's eyes filled with tears. She reached for me but I backed away. "Airy, please. You have to trust me. Fehin's father is a very bad man. He nearly killed me."

My mouth opened in surprise. "So that's what this is all about? I already know we're related, Mother. Fehin's mother told us. I thought you were friends with her."

"I am. I was. Brandubh kidnapped her, forced her to—"

I shook my head. "No. Gertrude told me that she loved Fehin's father. She said he had a dark side but he came out of it later. He changed."

My mother wiped the tears from her eyes. "Brandubh never came out of what you term his 'dark side' Airy. He tried to destroy Otherworld. I can't believe Gertrude would tell you she loved him! He held her hostage and had his way with her—that's how she got pregnant. Brandubh is your great great uncle, my grandmother, Catriona's, twin brother."

I scoffed. "If what you're worried about is deformed children, we aren't anywhere near such a decision. And besides, the familial connection isn't that close."

"Fehin looks just like him and has his blood, Airy. The man was a monster."

I turned from where we sat together on the park bench, noticing Fehin coming toward us from across the street. When he reached us he smiled and held out his hand. "Good morning Mrs. Fitzhugh."

My mother turned away, as though too disgusted to acknowledge his existence, making me furious. I stood up and stared down at her. "That's it, Mother. If you have no regard for Fehin then you have no regard for me." I grabbed Fehin's hand and pulled him toward the road. Before we left the grassy verge I stopped and called out, "And if you ever want a relationship with me you'll have to apologize and accept who I am!"

"What was all that about?" Fehin asked when we were half way across the street.

I let out a long sigh and waited until we'd dodged the cars and safely reached the other side before answering. "She seems to think that since your father did bad things that means you'll do bad things."

Fehin scoffed. "Yeah, he's Wolf's father too, and that dude was—"

"Seriously creepy," I finished for him. "Mom seems to be afraid that I'll get pregnant like she did."

Fehin laughed. "I get it now. She's afraid you'll follow in her footsteps."

"Hardly. She gave birth to me in Otherworld on the auspicious night of Lughnasa. I was born in a hut set up by the Crion and brought into the world with the help of fruit given to Mom by the moon goddess. Mom is like a goddess herself, a legend in Otherworld. How can she equate my life with hers? I have no—"

Fehin held up his hand. "Don't start that again. I don't want to hear how ordinary you are and how you have no gifts. I'm not sure why your parents gave you that impression—maybe to protect you? But come on, Airy—think about what we did last year."

I thought of the medicine wheel, the explosion of energy the two of us created--the bridge that connected worlds, or at least connected people. We'd started a revolution that hopefully would continue. But it hadn't changed the environmental damage that had already been done. I played with my ring, turning it around on my finger. It burned and throbbed as though waiting for me to use it. "I want to get out of here, Fehin. I want to see an earlier time and get away from my mother and anyone else who tries to come between us. My parents don't have the right to decide who I'm friends with, or who I choose to love."

Fehin lifted his eyebrows. "Are you saying you love me?"

I glanced at him. "You know how I feel about you. Stop fooling around."

Fehin's eyes lit on my moonstone ring, the one that had carried us through time on several past occasions. "You're talking serious time travel."

"Yes, I am."

It was a little over an hour later that we stood together in the woods behind the college. It was here that Fehin had first shared his magic with me, here that he'd kissed me the first time. It seemed fitting that we would leave from here. I stared down at my ring and pulled it off my finger. When I held it in my palm I could feel it pulsating as the magic built. "Are you ready?"

He ran his fingers through his long hair, pushing it back from his pale forehead. "As ready as I'll ever be," he smiled.

I took hold of his hand. "I want to go to medieval England!" I shouted, as though the gods of time-travel were so far away that I wouldn't be heard. A second later I felt weightless and closed my eyes against the dizzy feeling as we spun away.

Fehin righted himself from where he'd landed on his knees, rubbing them as he scanned the forest of trees around us. "Where did the ring take us?"

I tried to remember the layout of the woods we'd been in a minute before as I slipped the ring back on my finger, glancing at the innocuous pale orb before taking a look around. The scent of decaying wood, acorns, moss and damp earth rode on the light breeze, a creek murmuring in the distant gloom as though a conversation was going on just beyond our range. It was day, although there was barely any sky visible through the thick canopy. The leaves were green and dense, limbs spreading upward as though reaching for the heavens. Beneath the trees, shadows danced, changing from moment to moment as currents of air stirred the branches. A bird chirped in the distance, and another answered, the trilling calls echoing in the stillness. There was something different about the feel of the air, the scents, and the shape of the trees.

"This definitely isn't Milltown," Fehin said, echoing my own thoughts.

"I agree." I took in a deep breath, reveling in the clean scent of fresh air. "There are tons of animals here!"

"How do you know?"

"I just know." I scanned through the underbrush, seeing a bushy tail disappearing. In the twenty-first century too many chemicals had been dumped in the sea and on land, animals going extinct so fast it made your head spin. Big agriculture still used sprays that had been proven toxic to both humans and animals and yet nothing was being done about it. Bees had virtually disappeared and migrating birds were suffering as well. Corporations ruled, and the ones doing the worst for the environment were growing GMO crops that already had pesticides inside the seeds. Even the gray squirrels had lost ground, and the smaller red ones had nearly disappeared.

"Don't get your hopes up, Airy. If this is the fifth century people hunt for their food."

I pulled open the pack and took out my phone. "Cell phone doesn't work," I announced.

"Surprise, surprise," Fehin chuckled.

I heard laughter and then a man and a woman burst out from under the canopy on our right. The woman had leaves stuck in her thick chestnut hair and she was busy adjusting the bodice of her long medieval looking dress. A pale underskirt showed below the soft brown linen with the lace up front. They stopped dead when they saw us, staring in surprise. And then the man spoke in a deep brogue that was barely understandable.

"Merlin, where have ye been? What happened to your beard? The King's been askin' for ye. And what in Uther's name are you wearin'?" The man peered closer. "You look very rested for a man your age. Could it have anything to do with this comely lass next to ye, or is it a spell ye've cast to make yourself more appealin'?"

Fehin brushed at his jeans, but before he could reply there was a loud shout and the man and woman rushed into the brush in the other direction.

A moment later two men ran by, one of them glancing at us before coming to an abrupt halt. "Did ye by chance see a man wearin' blacksmith clothin' and a woman dressed in brown?" he asked, running agitated fingers through his shoulder-length hair.

"They went that way," I replied, pointing in the opposite direction from where they'd gone.

"That woman happens to be my wife," he growled, glancing at his companion. "She's a bedswerver and I will see her turned out and her head shaved for it."

"Shave her head because she's with another man?" I asked.

He stared, seeming to notice me for the first time. "She swore allegiance to me as wife and has now taken up with a peasant who sleeps in a barn!"

It was then I noticed his finer clothes, the long frockcoat made out of dark wool. "Was the marriage arranged?" I asked him.

His eyes narrowed. "What business is that of yours? If I had more time I'd take the two of ye into jail. Your speech is odd and ye have no right to be here in the king's woods." He peered closer to stare at Fehin. "Ye look suspiciously like the wizard that roams these parts. Tell me your name, boy!"

"He's Merlin," I answered quickly. "And if you aren't careful he'll turn you into a toad. If you want to catch your wife you'd best go now."

The man looked startled for a moment "I suppose I'll have to leave ye to it," he said, turning away. "But ye'd better not be poachin'. He glanced at his companion and then the two of them hurried off, disappearing into the gloom of the forest.

"So I'm to be Merlin in this timeline?" Fehin asked, amused.

I smirked. "Looks like it. I have to say you kind of fit the part. Maybe we can use your identity to explain why we're dressed so oddly."

"Well, come on then," Fehin said, pulling me by the hand. "We don't want to waste more time standing around in the woods."

"Waste time," I repeated, giggling. "I'd say we were *using* time, not wasting it."

We were walking along the rough dirt roadway when a carriage barreled up behind us, the horse neighing in protest as the driver pulled it to a hasty stop. "What have we here?" he asked, peering down at us.

I looked up at him, shading my eyes against the glare. "This is Merlin and I'm his apprentice. Can you give us a ride to town?"

"Merlin. You look nothing like the Merlin I know unless your magic allows ye to grow younger." He stared at us for a minute longer before saying, "Get in then."

When Fehin pulled opened the door the well-dressed man inside frowned, his eyes dark with annoyance. "What is the meaning of this!" he called out to the driver.

"I'm only giving them a ride to town, sir," the driver yelled back.

We climbed in and took the seat across from him.

"I suppose you are members of the magic troupe that comes through here," he said, eyeing our clothes suspiciously. "But I have never seen such outlandish outfits. I hesitate to be seen with you."

"So sorry, sir," Fehin said. "I am Merlin and we are dressed like this because we've come from the future. You do know that I am capable of such things? I hate to discommode you in any way, but we were not able to dress properly before we moved through the ether."

I stared at Fehin. Not only did he speak with an accent, the words he used and how he said them held surprising authority. Was magic at play here?

The man took this in, still frowning. "I am glad for your explanation, young wizard, but I would be pleased if you and your lady would disembark short of town so that I may be taken to my destination without fear of rumor."

"Of course," Fehin replied, before leaning out the window. "Driver, please let us off before town!" he yelled.

"Ye have it," came the reply.

I gazed out the window at the stretch of dark forest we traveled past. The air was thick with oxygen, deer grazing here and there in the lush meadows between spreading branches of beech trees. To our left the ground rose gradually, and at the very top a group of standing stones stood together, sentinels conferring on important matters. I wondered if we were in Wales, the country where Merlin was purported to have his home. I hesitated to ask.

Church spires appeared in the distance and then the crenellated towers of a magnificent castle presented itself at the top of another hill. An arrangement of thatched roofs became visible in the hollow below as we drew closer—the village. The coach came to an abrupt halt. "'Tis merely a mile or two," he said when we left the carriage. "T'will do ye both good." He laughed, his whip falling on the horse's flank. The carriage rattled away, the horse moving into a fast trot.

"Our friend didn't even say goodbye," I said.

"I'm sure he was glad to see us go."

"How can we find other clothes to wear? I should have thought about that before we left Milltown."

Fehin shrugged. "I'm a magician, remember? What we wear is of little significance."

I scoffed. "Good luck with that. From my readings I always thought Merlin was a fictional character. How come those people accepted you?"

"Do you believe every supposed historical fact you read? Do you think regular people in the twenty-first century would believe I came from the distant future, conjured an island, and am friends with the god Loki? What about my dragons?"

I chuckled. "Yeah. They wouldn't believe my history either."

"Merlin may merely be a magician who travels through villages doing magic tricks," Fehin continued.

"Then why did the man in the woods mention Uther?"

Fehin shrugged. "Maybe he's in the king's employ."

I chuckled. "You sure get with the local lingo quickly, Merlin," I said, impressed with the speech patterns. We reached the outskirts of town and exchanged a look. "Let's go to the market and see if we can..."

"Steal some clothes?" Fehin asked, grinning. "I'm good with that sort of thing."

"This is a talent I never knew about."

"Yes, well, I haven't had much reason to use it. Follow closely, and if I run, run with me." He raised his eyebrows, his mouth quirking.

The market was filled with the bustle of people doing their weekly shopping, the pungent stench of pigs and horse manure, squawking chickens, and everyone shouting their wares and grabbing gawkers by their sleeves to entice them to buy. I stepped in something I was sure was not mud, trying to wipe off my shoe as I stumbled after Fehin. Once inside the throng we were barely noticed in the hubbub.

The smell of frying fish and fresh baked bread wafted toward me as I strolled along the stalls admiring baskets, hand woven shawls in natural dyes, and knitted hats and gloves. If I had the money of the time I would have purchased something, but I only had modern coin and a few dollar bills. Behind me were the sausage makers, and next to them were the fishmongers, freshly caught trout staring up with glassy eyes.

I was admiring painted clay beads when I saw Fehin dart away, coming back a few moments later with clothing in his arms. He raised his eyebrows, signaling for me to follow. We had moved away from the main market area when a large hand clamped down on my shoulder.

"And where do you two think you're going?" the man asked. "Stealing is a capital offence. Ye could be hanged."

A frisson of fear moved through me before I noticed the lines of humor around a mouth that seemed ready to break into laughter. Gray hair hung in tangles next to a face shaped very much like Fehin's, the eyes exactly the same forest green.

"Are you Merlin?" I whispered.

"Ye guessed my name. And from what I can tell I have a doppelganger."

Fehin stared at him with an expression I'd never seen on his face. "You do exist," he said quietly.

Merlin laughed. "And why wouldn't I?"

"Because you're a myth in the future," I supplied, watching Fehin out of the corner of my eye. After his little history lesson I was surprised to see him so taken aback.

"In the future—is that where the two of ye emerged from? T'would explain the manner of dress."

"We traveled from twenty-first century America. The continent was peopled with natives until the British settled there in the sixteen-hundreds," I had to explain for some reason.

Merlin nodded. "I know of this."

"You see the future?" Fehin asked.

"In a manner of speaking." He looked around. "We should get ye dressed in the proper attire before the authorities drag ye to the dungeons as witches come from the underworld."

But before we managed to get very far another man joined us, and this one did not have a smile on his craggy features. "Merlin, I should have your head for what ye've been up to. And what's this then? Two of yours?"

Maybe we should go now, I heard Fehin say in my head.

But what about Merlin—don't you want...?

My attention came back to what was going on between the two men, realizing that Merlin was about to be arrested and us with him. We could either trust in the wizard's magic or trust in our own.

Take us out of here—we can come back and find him later.

I grabbed Fehin's arm and moved us through the ether again. And this time when we landed the woods was made up of entirely different trees, species I hadn't seen before, and the air did not smell fresh. Fehin's eyebrows pulled together as he tried to right himself from where he'd fallen. "That was abrupt."

I pursed my lips and stared at him. "You're the one who told me to do it."

"I didn't say a thing."

"I heard you in my head, Fehin. You distinctly told me to get us out of there."

Fehin stared at me. "And I'm telling you I didn't."

"Well, then, who did?"

Fehin shrugged. "The only explanation is Merlin. He was afraid for us."

"But how would he know about the ring, or—?"

"He's a wizard, just like me, but way more powerful." His eyes went dark. "Medieval England is a violent place. I hope you realize what we're getting into. Where exactly did you take us this time?"

"I'm not entirely sure. I think I said something like 'get us out of here'."

"Well, that's really specific. Maybe we're on the moon."

"Very funny, Fehin. At least the people in the past don't have nuclear bombs, drones, and assault rifles on every corner. I'll take my chances with bows and arrows. Maybe I'll learn to be an archer."

"That is if the stone didn't take us into a timeline that has those things. We could be anywhere. You need to learn how to work that thing."

"Thanks very much for your vote of confidence. At least I saved us from jail."

"Or Merlin did."

"Oh yeah, Merlin, the mythological figure of Camelot fame." I giggled at the absurdity of what we were doing and then both of us turned giddy, laughing so hard we had to sit down. We quieted when we heard the neigh of a horse and the clatter of wheels. Whoever it was drew close, paused for a moment, and then moved by, the rattling diminishing until it was gone. "Sounds like the same timeline," I whispered.

Fehin pressed his lips together and shrugged. "Maybe, maybe not. There are carts in nearly every timeline, even ours."

I scoffed, "Only out in the country around the farming areas."

Fehin made a face. "And does this seem like a bustling city, my little time traveling guru?"

I ignored him, my attention going to the woods. There was an odd odor here that I couldn't identify. The trees looked perfectly normal, although there didn't seem to be much animal or insect life, and I didn't notice any acorns or leaf detritus under them, or any plants around them. In fact the entire area seemed too clean aide from caches of nuts stacked up in various places. Had squirrels done that? But I had yet to see or hear an animal of any kind. I noticed something shiny and bent to take a look. "Does this look medieval?"

"What is it?"

"It's a coin, one I've never seen before."

Fehin came close, examining the thin disc with the stylized swirls and rendering of a naked man running. "It's not odd that you haven't seen one like it—do you think museums or history books have pictures of every coin ever made?"

"True, but what manner of people would make a coin with a naked man as the design?"

Fehin took it in his fingers, turning it over to examine the back where a stylized bow and arrow had been etched into the paper-thin metal. "I don't know, Airy—maybe people who spend time running? There are cultures like that, you know. I'm no expert but I've never seen metal like this. I don't think it's copper or silver or platinum. It's not nickel or stainless steel or titanium either. He tried to bend it. "And it's really strong." He looked up. "Do you think we're in some future time?"

I scoffed. "You certainly aren't Merlin if you can ask a question like that."

Fehin chuckled, one hand pushing the shock of black hair off his face. "I guess we'll find out when we venture forth from the forest."

I stared at his profile in the shaded dusky light. His body was angular, his shoulders strong. When he turned, brown/green eyes met mine, dark against his pale Scottish skin. I thought he was beautiful and never tired of looking at him. The two of us together were quite a sight—me with my bright red curls, ruddy skin and freckles next to his paleness and hair that reminded me of raven's feathers. He looked like an appealingly handsome vampire, but that was only because I'd become obsessed with them after reading Bram Stoker, Stephen King, and Anne Rice and watching True Blood.

I sighed, bringing my attention back to the present. If Fehin was right, my ability to choose the ring's destination was sadly lacking. I shook my head, laughing to myself.

"This Merlin thing was your fantasy, not mine," Fehin said, noticing my mirth.

"You look like Merlin. That guy even said so. And after meeting the real Merlin I'm inclined to agree. And you're a wizard. You conjured an island."

"Yeah, I guess I did. But that was in the future. In Milltown it was a lot harder to do magic and sometimes it didn't work at all."

"That's because the atmosphere is too polluted. But despite that we managed to change things."

"Changed things? I know something happened, but as far as any of it sticking, I don't know. There's too much push-back."

"We started a movement, Fehin, It will either keep going or it won't. Do you want to go back and try and do more? We can if you want." I stared at him, daring him to come up with a plan of his own.

He shook his head. "I'd rather be on a time-travel adventure with you. It's too hard trying to fix the twenty-first century."

"Maybe if we stop some stuff from happening in the past it can help the future."

He let out a roar of laughter. "You are a true optimist, Airy."

As we wandered the woods we heard carts trundling by, the shouts of men and women yelling to small children who refused to behave. Two men arrived in the woods to take a leak, and if it hadn't been for my quick maneuvers they would have seen us. All I had to do was take us five minutes into the future to elude them—the first time I'd managed to do it right.

Something about this place didn't feel right. I'd seen caches of nuts and water in several places now and wondered what it was for. I was sure there were no animals living here. I didn't look forward to night. "We have to make a plan. We can't just wander around like a couple of zombies."

Fehin suppressed a laugh. "That word doesn't exist in this time, Airy. Try not to use twenty-first century slang when we're conversing with our medieval compatriots."

"We don't know for sure where we are in time, Fehin. We have to go out there to figure it out." I pointed toward where the tree line ended, a hazy glare emanating from what lay beyond. "I think we should probably get out of the woods before night comes. I don't like the feel of it and the trees won't tell me anything."

"Why not?" He turned to run his hand over the bark. "I've never felt bark like this," he said, scratching at it with his thumbnail.

I put my hand next to his, trying to get some response. "What the...?" My mouth fell open in surprise. "Fehin, these trees aren't even real! No wonder they won't speak to me!"

"What?" He bent to look at the bark again. "You're right. I thought it felt weird, but I figured it was some species we weren't familiar with. Why would there be fake trees?"

I scanned the area, noticing for the first time how straight all the trunks were and how the trees were perfectly spaced, their leaves all the same size and shape. A sinking sensation entered my stomach, filling me with dread. "I can't believe I didn't notice this. I don't like it, Fehin."

"Let's get out of here and take a look."

I grabbed his arm, suddenly frightened. "We need to be careful."

"If things get weird just take us away."

"To do that we have to be touching." I felt better when he twined his fingers through mine and led the way.

From the edge of the fake forest a flat plain, devoid of life, stretched toward the horizon. Wide roads paved in an unidentifiable substance ran here and there, coming together before disappearing over a hill into what seemed to be a steep canyon. The ground beyond the road was cracked and parched, as though there hadn't been rain in a very long time, and it went on and on, clumps of darkness suggesting more fake forests. A group of naked men and women ran by a hundred feet away from us, one of them glancing back before disappearing into the forest.

"I told you they were runners," Fehin said, watching them.

"They didn't seem very happy about it," I replied.

"You think they were running from something?"

I shrugged. "I don't know, but the expressions I could make out from this distance didn't seem joyful."

Fehin smirked. "Maybe they were playing strip poker, lost their clothes and decided to spend the night in the woods."

"Very funny."

A hazy and unhappy sun hung over the landscape, bringing oppressive heat that seemed responsible for the arid look of everything. I lifted the damp curls off my neck. "I could use a drink of water."

"Should have gotten a drink in the first world. This one seems devoid of moisture."

"Except those hollowed out logs filled with it. Did you notice them? But it didn't look very clean."

We hung back in the shadows watching the vehicles made of wood and canvas, and possibly metal, traveling the roads. Horses pulled some, others pulled by burly bearded men naked to the waist, and others moved mechanically on their own. The covered carts held men and women dressed in outlandish costumes in bright colors that belonged in a medieval masquerade ball, hats with feathers perched high on heads. The women had masses of hair configured into intricate braids and weavings, the men mostly bald. The carts that weren't covered were filled with dark skinned people wearing loose woven tunics, hair disheveled from the breeze as they rode by.

I stared in disbelief. "Where in hell are we?"

"How do I know? You're the one who brought us here."

I frowned, annoyed by his tone. "We need to find out, but walking along the road seems risky. Maybe if we work our way in the direction everyone seems to be heading we'll find a town." I pointed toward where all the roads converged in the far distance.

The ground where the fake trees had been placed was absolutely level, apparently man-made like the trees. We moved along the edge, keeping a wary eye on the vehicles and staying out of sight. Along the way I noticed more hollowed out logs either filled with water or nuts, some containing withered apples and pears. "Have you noticed any life out here?" I asked Fehin, pointing one out.

He bent down. "The only life I've seen is the people. Maybe the food and water is for them."

"You think they live out here?" I shook my head. "This is too weird."

27

When the trees abruptly ended I stared out at the open landscape. I glanced at Fehin. "Now what do we do? Maybe it's time to find another place to go." I took my ring off, ready to take us out of here if Fehin said the word.

"Don't you want to see what lies beyond that hill? I do."

We watched the vehicles disappearing from view one hundred yards ahead, the clatter of the horses hooves and rattle of the wheels fading. Beyond the yawning abyss the landscape swept up into reddish peaks and down into more valleys, the haze obliterating what lay beyond.

Fehin stared into the distance. "I say we wait until dark and hope that the traffic is gone by then."

Since the trees were fake there was no wood to be had for a fire, and as far as food, we didn't have much. I don't know why I hadn't thought to bring more. We munched on some sticks of jerky and potato chips and waited for dark to fall. Luckily the temperature remained warm. When night came, it seemed like a dense black curtain fell over the landscape. "Since I can't even see your face I think we can go now," I whispered, moving toward the small opening between two of the trees.

"Did you think to bring candles?"

"No. Did you?" I asked sarcastically. What was I, the tour director? "And can't you start fire with your fingers or something?"

Fehin waved his hands in the air, mumbling some words. "Doesn't work here," he said after a minute or two.

"Why not?"

"How do I know?"

"It would make me feel better if it did," I said. "But at least we have the ring." I grabbed his hand. "Let's go. If we don't get a move on we'll be up all night."

"Are you expecting to find a motel?" he asked, chuckling.

"I don't know. Maybe. I have no idea what we'll find. From what we've seen so far there could be anything down there."

"True enough," he said, pulling me with him toward the road.

We left the safety of the trees and moved to the road, checking both ways before heading for the canyon. Somehow the road was was lit from beneath. It dipped and twisted, a snake of light heading downward in a steady zigzag configuration. Beyond the light, shadows pressed and swelled, dark ridges indicating more valleys in the distance. A haze of dim light lit up what could be a large city, but it was hard to tell. The sky seemed as hazy as it had during the day, with no stars visible and no moon.

"Is this the Grand Canyon?" I asked.

"Could be. It certainly has similar topography."

"If it is I wonder what year we landed in—there was never a city this size here in the past, and I thought it was mostly Native Americans living in the canyon itself."

"Your guess is as good as mine," Fehin replied. "But a couple hundred years either way could account for it."

We walked side by side along the road. Several times I noticed naked men run by, heading for the woods, and once I saw a lone woman, her hair matted and tangled, her eyes wild, sprinting toward the fake trees. There was no traffic and no sounds whatsoever except the occasional horn that sounded like one used by foxhunters, and the one high-pitched scream that echoed into the distance.

"What was that?"

Fehin shrugged and moved ahead of me. I hurried after him, nervous.

Once the road dipped lower into the canyon, tall spires and stone buildings and bridges came into view, lit by what could only be street lamps. "This is odd,"Fehin said, squinting into the distance. "Now it looks like we're in a medieval city, and yet…"

"And yet this doesn't look like Europe. Maybe this is the future. The pavement is made of some material I've never seen before, and where have you ever seen lights like this underneath a road?"

"I thought we were heading into the past, Airy. If we're in the future all bets are off."

"All bets for what? What difference does it make?"

"Only that if it's the future we're in unchartered territory. Anything could be going on here."

Once the road leveled out and just before the outskirts to the city, a wide river appeared, murky water running sluggishly by as though it could barely get up the energy to move. We slowed to a walk to cross the high medieval bridge of gray stone and headed up the road on the other side. My eyes burned from exhaustion. "Shall we find a place to spend the rest of the night?"

Fehin scanned from one side of the road to the other. "There's no place to hide. I think we should keep going. Cities have doorways, and there are churches and alleys where we could sleep for an hour or two."

I viewed the lights in the distance. The buildings were either medieval stone or shockingly modern, the modern ones made of some shiny material, like glass or metal. The edges were sharp and not at all inviting, jagged spires reaching into the starless sky. "Most cities have those things, but I'm not sure this one does."

He didn't respond as I followed him up the hill and around a bend. The city was not far, but I didn't feel inclined to enter that mass of uninviting structures. When we came to a small grove of fake trees, I stopped. "I have to rest, Fehin." I headed off the roadway and found a tree to lean against, sinking down and resting my head against the strange rubbery bark. "If the people we saw were the norm there's no way we can blend in. I'm not sure what to do when it gets light."

Fehin sat cross-legged across from me. "That's why I wanted to get into the city while it's still dark. Get some sleep. It does wonders for the thinking process."

Despite my exhaustion, when I closed my eyes I couldn't sleep, and lay awake wondering why I hadn't insisted we move to another time line. I finally admitted to myself that there was something intriguing about it all; I wanted to find out where we were and what year it was. Why were the trees fake and who were those wildly dressed people? And what about the naked people who seemed to be living in the woods? What we'd seen so far did not match anything in any history book I'd ever read. And if it was the future I wanted to discover *when* it was.

We were awakened by the clatter of wheels on the road, our gaze meeting in the pre-dawn light. "Seems like the natives get started early," Fehin whispered, moving close.

When I leaned forward to check out the road, there was a shout, and a moment later a man and a woman were glaring down at us. I stared up into two faces contorted with anger.

CHAPTER TWO

FEHIN

"Who are you?" the man asked, reaching out to haul Airy to her feet.

I quickly pushed myself to standing and was about to grab her away from him, when the man cuffed me hard, sending me reeling backward. "I asked a question," he growled, staring at Airy.

"I—we, came from--" she looked at me.

"We came from back there," I supplied, gesturing toward the road leading upward behind us.

The man shook his head, glancing at his companion. "What do you think, Ing?"

They were dressed in loose fitting cotton muslin, dyed a rich shade of indigo. The woman wore a long skirt under her hip length tunic, and the man wore trousers. Their feet were encased in handmade leather sandals. Both had dark skin, dark hair and eyes, and appeared to be of either Asian or middle-eastern descent. "I do not know what to think," the woman replied, looking us over. "They do not resemble anyone I know, and their clothing is odd. We have been worried about invaders from the east, could they be scouts?" She grabbed my arm and turned it over to peer at my inside wrist. "She has no tattoo."

The man grabbed my wrist. "Neither does he. You're coming with us," he said, digging in his pocket to pull out a rope. He quickly tied our hands and pulled us forward toward the road.

"Where are we?" Airy asked.

The woman swiveled to stare at her. "This is one of the largest cities on the planet. Canhavu is world-renowned for its trade. Sailing ships arrive daily from foreign ports and the big ones once a month. How can you not know that?" Her eyes narrowed suspiciously.

"I—we got lost in the forest."

She laughed. "That is impossible. There is nothing for miles and has not been for over a hundred years. You have no wheels—you would have been killed with the rest of them." She tipped up Airy's chin with her forefinger. "Now tell me, where did you really come from?"

I could see the panic on Airy's face, but before she could answer a covered cart came barreling down the road and nearly ran into us. Wide-eyed, the driver pulled on the reins too hard and the horse lost its balance, careening off the road and taking the cart with it. The horse came to a stop, neighing frantically when the cart turned over. The man inside crawled out, his plump face red with anger. In the meantime the driver undid the stays and released the frightened beast, which ran off under the fake trees.

"What is the meaning of this?" the passenger demanded, his gaze going from one to the other. "And who are these prisoners? You have no jurisdiction here."

The man was dressed in a red frockcoat decorated with gold braid, a hat of the same color on his head. His manner was officious--maybe a magistrate of some kind.

The man and woman glanced at one another. "We found these two lurking here. They have no tattoos. We are taking them to the city to find out who they are."

He looked our captors up and down, seeming to take in their clothing, which was very different from his own. "I suggest you hand them over to me. It is obvious to the most unskilled observer that you have no authority whatsoever." He turned to call to his driver who was busy dealing with the horse. "I am a busy man!" he yelled. "Get this contraption righted and back on the road!"

The man and woman handed the rope over that tied us together, and hurried off to the cart they'd left on the other side of the road. Theirs was uncovered and more rustic looking, the creature who pulled it, small and skinny. By the expression in their eyes they were glad to get away from our new oppressor.

More carts clattered past as the driver managed to right the carriage and get the horse back into his traces. The man in red held onto the rope with his right hand, tapping his foot in impatience. "Hurry, would you please? I don't have all day to stand around here."

Two carts moved past pulled by men, sweat glistening on their naked upper bodies. "I should have hired one of those," Red Coat said, pointing. "At least they don't have accidents."

Once the cart was ready to go Red Coat pulled us with him into the carriage, pointing toward the city. "May as well return," he told the driver. "I'll have to bring these two in for questioning before I go hunting."

"What is there to hunt?" I asked.

The man laughed. "Indigents like yourselves, of course. Did you think we still had animals? You're lucky I didn't find you two when you were supposedly lost in those woods," he laughed. "That's free hunting land for those who have a license. Under law I have to bring you in, but with any luck you'll be released into the wild again." He took hold of a lock of Airy's hair and pulled her around so he could peer at her. "On second thought maybe the brothel might be a good fit. People enjoy the young ones." He let out a bark of laughter. "I just might have the perfect place if I don't decide to keep you for myself."

When I glanced toward Airy her eyes were wide with fear. In my mind I heard her say, *we have to get out of here*. But I knew unless she could touch me I would be left behind. I was on one seat and she was on the other—too far to reach, especially with our hands tied. *Go, Airy. I'll be ok*, I answered. But she shook her head and turned to stare out the window where cart after cart of people dressed in indigo cotton passed us, heading the other way. They had crossbows on their laps as though going hunting. I counted at least a dozen of them, every rustic cart filled to capacity.

The city was amazing, and if I hadn't been scared shitless I would have been drinking it in. Each building seemed to outdo the one before, all of them either medieval in nature, made from gray stone with mullioned windows and several chimneys, or glass and metal with sharp edges and towers and turrets and spires that reached high into the sky. In between the enormous skyscrapers were rows of what I thought must be housing clustered into stacked apartments and painted in pinks, turquoise, and lime green, windows like wide eyes facing outward to take in the busy street. The streets were filled with carts, sellers next to the road hawking their wares, the bustle and din of activity filling the air. "I seriously dislike market day," Red Coat muttered, looking out. "Glad the ships only come once a month."

"What about the sailing ships?" Airy asked.

He turned, seeming surprised to hear her speak. "They arrive from closer ports and they have little in the way of goods to trade, although we sometimes get a box of exotic fruit or an animal to use as a pet. They are usually eaten within a week or so after the children tire of playing with them." He turned to look out the window.

Airy's face crumpled and turned the color of chalk. I wanted to comfort her but there was nothing I could do. I tried to see what was being sold as we trundled by, noting the bags of rice and beans of different kinds. "Fresh killed today!" the man in indigo standing behind a table of meat called out. "Get it before it's gone!" Beyond the first tier of carts I noticed several naked and dejected men and women chained together along one side. Slaves? They were dark haired with nutmeg colored skin like the ones who wore indigo, whereas the brighter clothing seemed to be worn by paler people, with brown or blonde hair. They were the ones who walked along the streets purchasing things. I hadn't noticed the skin color of the runners we saw in early dusk, but I had a feeling it was dark.

Pants, skirts and jackets in stripes and rainbow colors made up another booth, another filled with the indigo tunics and trousers. I saw beads of glass and bracelets made of the same gold material as the coin, women selling what looked like handcuffs in silver and gold colored metals. Bows and arrows made of fine wood and others made of the rubbery material like the trees filled another booth where shoppers crowded close. Hunting seemed to be a national pastime.

We passed by the market area and came into a quieter section of town where stone buildings stood like squat creatures, their sad gray faces lit up in the last rays of the sun. "I've decided to forego any formalities with you two," Red Coat announced, tapping on the ceiling of the carriage. "Let them come and get me if they don't like it." He laughed as if he'd made a joke.

The conveyance came to an abrupt stop in front of one of the houses and our 'host' exited the carriage, pulling us along with him. He gave a cursory wave to the driver and dragged us up the stone steps and into the house that shared walls with the houses on either side. It was stone but seemed newer than the others we'd seen. But the roof still sported two chimneys and smoke was coming out of one of them.

"I feel sick," Airy announced as soon as we were inside. I glanced at her, wondering if this was a ploy, but her skin was still chalk-like and her eyes were watery. I knew she suffered from motion sickness.

"If you plan to vomit on my floor you'll be cleaning it yourself, "Red Coat said, frowning. He untied her and dragged her down a dimly lit hallway and opened a door.

As soon as I heard her retching I realized the danger of what we were doing. It wasn't just the man who had captured us--it was this place and the aura that surrounded it. "What do you plan to do with us?" I asked.

He chuckled. "The same things that happen to anyone of your class. And no tattoo gives me the freedom to decide your fate for myself. You're not in the system so I have free rein."

"What kind of fate are we talking about? I can help you with some stuff—I have magic."

He peered at me. "Is that so? Then why was it so easy to catch you? I need to get you two cleaned up so I can get a better look at you. You could bring me a lot of money. That is if I don't find another use for you." His eyes glinted as he leered at me.

I had a momentary terror that I pushed down. This man was a pervert. Maybe everyone here was a pervert—I had no idea. Judging from what I'd seen at the market, human beings were not held in high esteem. Where in hell were we? "I thought you said we'd be released into the wild."

His thick rubbery lips moved into a smile. "That would only happen if I took you to the authorities. No, I think I'll play with you a while before I do that."

"Airy is sick. She'll need to rest."

"Airy? What a nice name. And you are...?"

"Fehin, my name's Fehin."

"Well, Fehin, despite your insistence that you have magic I would suggest giving up control over your future. You belong to me now."

Airy came out of the bathroom and walked unsteadily toward us.

"Better now?" the man asked.

She nodded, her gaze going to the floor.

"All right then." He let out a bellow, bringing a maid running.

The young woman was around eighteen, dark hair pulled back in a braid. She looked Asian, maybe part Chinese, and was dressed in a black uniform. "Yes, sir?" she asked, her fearful gaze darting to the two of us.

"Take these two up to the maid's quarters and get them cleaned up. I want them back down in the drawing room and ready to be examined when you've finished. And hurry, please. I might still have time to take them to auction."

She curtsied before nodding to us to follow her down the hall and into a narrow stairwell that spiraled upward. "What is this place?" Airy asked, hurrying after her.

"It is the place of your worst nightmares," she answered, going ahead of us up the steps.

Airy met my gaze, her eyes filled with tears. I reached to take her hand but the maid grabbed hold of her and twisted her away. "No touching," she said sharply.

When we reached the top floor she led us down yet another long hallway and opened a door at the end. "You in here," she said, pulling Airy's arm to shove her inside. "Wash, and when you're finished press the bell on the wall." She closed the door and locked it, putting the key in her pocket. A few doors down and on the other side of the hall she opened a door into another bathroom and ushered me inside. "Do as you're told and things will go a lot better," she said.

"But what will he do with us—what does he want?"

She shook her head, her eyes going dark. "Just listen and don't ask too many questions. Mr. Sand is not the worst master I've ever had, but he has his dark side, and believe me, you do not want to see that part of him." She closed the door and I heard the lock click.

I took off my clothes and turned on the tap, my mind scattering everywhere at once as I waited for the tub to fill. I went over to what I thought was a window, discouraged when I found a flat piece of material that housed some sort of light behind it. I sent another message to Airy. *Don't worry—we'll find a way out of here.* But there was no answer. Either she was too terrified to send and receive telepathic messages or she was sick again. I worried as I lowered myself into the steaming water. I had to get more information out of the maid—she was the only one we could talk to. And how had she known to keep us from touching? If we'd managed to clasp hands we wouldn't be in this predicament. I dreaded facing our captor, my mind conjuring all sorts of scenarios, each one worse than the one before. What kind of examining did he have in mind? I shuddered to think. I had to find a way to protect Airy.

CHAPTER THREE
AIRY

The bathroom floor was made of small hexagonal black and white tiles that I'd seen in modern bathrooms and also older houses dating back to the eighteen hundreds. The tub was a claw foot, another older design that hadn't lost its popularity. The fixtures were made of a metal I couldn't identify. There was nothing in here to indicate *when* we were in time. The market had given me the sense that we were in the past, but now I wasn't so sure, especially with the glass and metal buildings I'd seen. I couldn't remember what I'd been thinking when I instructed the stone.

I shivered in the cooling water wondering what to do. This was obviously a dangerous place where human beings were treated like animals. And this man was not a good man. One part of me wanted to disappear as quickly as I could, but the other part refused to leave Fehin. If I left here I 'd never find him again.

When I stepped out of the tub and rang the bell I'd resolved to question the maid. Even though she seemed brusque, she was my only hope.

When the lock clicked and the door swung open she handed me a robe. "Put this on," she ordered.

I turned my back to drop my towel. "What year is it?" I asked as I pulled on the robe.

"The year? How would I know? I am merely a slave."

"You don't keep records or know how long you've been working here, or—?"

She shook her head impatiently. "It makes no difference. Each day is basically the same. My life will go on like this until I die."

"Don't you want a better life?"

"Of course I do. But if I escaped I would only end up being hunted out on the plains with the rest of them."

"Why don't you find another town, another place to live?"

She scoffed, her dark eyes meeting mine as I turned to face her. "This city is the only one for hundreds of miles, maybe thousands. I've never seen any other town or city. I was born here and I will die here. My life is better than the ones who are hunted."

"What happens to them?"

"What do you think? They are killed."

I put my hand up to my mouth and barely made it to the toilet before I brought up the rest of the contents of my stomach.

She came behind me and pulled my hair back as I continued to retch. "Where are you from? You don't seem to understand the ways here," she said gently.

I sat back on the tiled floor, spent and exhausted. "Fehin and I are from another time. We traveled here from the future or the past—I don't know which because I don't know what year it is here. Are there any animals alive besides horses?"

She shook her head. "The horses are bred specially for pulling the carts and fed a diet that keeps them alive. Any others were gone long before my time."

"What do you eat?"

"The ships bring foodstuffs from other parts of the globe—rice and beans and soybeans and vegetables, although they are none too fresh by the time they arrive."

"And is the society divided into those who have a lot of money and slaves, or is there another class in the middle?"

"It is people like us and people like Mr. Sand. There is no middle."

"What about homeless, or people who can't afford to—"

"There are no homeless. They are hunted long before that. I don't know this to be true, but I have the sense that their meat is sold to the very wealthy. It is seen as a delicacy."

I gagged as I remembered the meat in the market, the call of 'fresh killed today'. It couldn't be, I said to myself, attempting to get hold of my fear.

The maid didn't seem concerned as she continued in a monotone. "The master will be angry if we don't make haste. Wait here for one moment while I check on your friend."

"Wait. Do you have a toothbrush—toothpaste?"

She looked blank for a moment before she registered what I meant. "There," she said, pointing to a cabinet set into the wall.

I hoped she would leave the door open but instead she closed and locked it. I opened the cabinet and pulled out a little brush that hadn't been used and a can of what could only be tooth powder and proceeded to brush my teeth, my tongue and every other part of my mouth. I rinsed six times with water.

A few minutes later I heard footsteps and the door opened. Fehin stood behind her dressed in a brown robe similar to mine, his hair still wet. "Come along now. If you do as the master asks you will have a meal later."

We followed her down the dark hall, our gaze meeting in the gloom.

After hearing about the hunting I could not imagine putting any food in my stomach. *What is wrong, Airy? Why didn't you answer me?* I heard Fehin ask.

I didn't hear you ask anything. They hunt humans, Fehin. We have to get out of here.

I know.

What can we do?

We'll have to wait for an opportunity to touch.

What if we don't get one?

But Fehin didn't answer as we were ushered into the drawing room. Mr. Sand stood with his back to the cold and empty fireplace. Without any real wood I wondered what they burned.

"There you are! And scrubbed clean. Please disrobe so I can examine you for lice and other blemishes and vermin that might impede your sales."

Fehin removed his robe, his eyes pleading with me to do the same. I moved closer to him, noticing the avid look on Mr. Sand's face as he waited for me to obey. *Get ready.*

"Take off your robe, girl!" Mr. Sand shouted a second later, reaching toward me. But instead of doing what he asked I flung myself at Fehin, knocking him to the floor as I said the words to take us out of there.

⤳

"Where are we?" I heard Fehin mutter. "And why do we always end up in a dark forest in the middle of the night?"

"Somewhere not there," I gasped, my stomach churning. "I said *early times*, I think. Honestly, I don't even know. All I could think about was getting away from Mr. Sand!"

Fehin reached out in the dark and pulled me to him.

"You don't have your robe," I said stupidly. "You're naked and I'm wearing a flimsy piece of cotton. If we're in a medieval town somewhere we're going to be in even more trouble."

"At least we won't be running for our lives," he said, planting a kiss on my mouth.

I pulled away. "Now is not the time for that—we need to figure out what we're doing."

He snorted. "What do you have in mind, Airy? Another foray into a medieval world that isn't medieval? Or should we give up and go back to Milltown?"

"We didn't come prepared. We need costumes of the time, and food."

Fehin laughed. "Except you never know where we'll end up. That one was a doozy. What we need is more control, ring girl."

"That's what I'm talking about. I need to figure out how to do this without sending us to another horrible place like that. I don't know what I could have said in my mind to end up there. I'm sure it was way in the future after every animal has gone extinct. As far as I could tell there weren't even any plants, except what comes on the ships."

"I saw a bunch of rice and bags of different beans at the market. Maybe they grow them in greenhouses. When you think about it they have a pretty good system going. No homeless, no impoverished."

"Oh yeah. Hunting the homeless sounds wonderful."

He laughed humorlessly. "At least they aren't starving on the streets. But I'm glad we didn't stay long enough to join them."

"This is serious, Fehin. The maid said she's heard rumors that the hunted who are killed are sold as meat to the really wealthy. That is so disgusting that I can barely imagine it. Is this the result of what we're doing in our time? We can't let the world turn into this!"

"Airy, calm down. We don't even know where we were, or when. And don't trust what the maid said—she was probably trying to freak you out."

"I wish we hadn't left Merlin's world. I'm taking us back to Milltown where we can study the environment and find out how to help. I seriously can't stand it!" Tears squeezed out of the corners of my eyes and a minute later I was sobbing.

"Jesus, Airy. This was supposed to be fun."

"If you think being in a place like that was fun then I don't want to be your friend anymore."

Fehin grabbed my arm. "That is not what I meant. I suppose we should have been prepared, but I wouldn't have believed it if I hadn't been there. Faced with a world like that I just don't think two people can make much of a difference."

"Isn't that what you said when we went to the medicine wheel? And look how that turned out. We can't change anything if we don't try." I placed my hands on the wide trunk next to me. "This is a real tree."

"What does it say?"

I gasped, pulling my hands away. "It says we need to get out of here, that this is a very dangerous place."

Fehin laughed. "Trees do not have the same concerns humans do. Maybe it's talking about being cut down or burned. I say we take a look around before we take off again."

I had my fingers on the ring ready to whisk us away. "You may be right. What harm will it do to take a look? We can always leave if things get dicey. But Fehin, you're naked."

"Maybe I can steal some clothes." He headed away, shafts of moonlight casting a glow across his pale body as he moved like a wraith through the woods.

"It's a good thing it's warm," I muttered, following him.

CHAPTER FOUR
FEHIN

Once we were out of the forest we faced a landscape of vast rolling hills of grass, the tips silvery in the moonlight as they waved in the light breeze. Other woodland areas stood dark here and there, herds of animals ambling along as they grazed. "Doesn't look very dangerous to me," I said, turning to Airy.

But she was laughing, her gaze on my bare butt. "Aren't you embarrassed?" she asked.

I scanned the empty landscape. "Who's going to see me? And anyway, I don't find nakedness particularly embarrassing. I used to go naked all the time on Thule."

"When you were a kid."

"And when I was older. All of us did, even the ones in their sixties and seventies and older."

"So you grew up a nudist?" She was laughing again, her entire body shaking.

"We didn't refer to it as that—it was just what we did. Now stop laughing and get serious. I think I see fires in the distance."

She followed my gaze. "What do you think it is?"

I shrugged. "Could be camps. Maybe the people here cook over an open fire. Could explain the tree's worry. Didn't you say you used the word primitive?"

"*Early times.* Guess it's about the same. Are those buffalo?" She pointed to the large shapes in the distance.

"Could be. They're big enough. Maybe this is early America before the white man took over."

"I hope so," she answered, scanning moodily into the distance.

I guess she didn't realize how the tribes interacted. From what I'd read there were constant wars over land, disagreements related to trade and women; all sorts of things. The noble savage was true only up to a point. And we were white-skinned--not their favorite people. "I say we rest in the woods over there until the sun comes up. I have a feeling the Indians might not take kindly to two white people arriving in the middle of the night."

"Especially a naked one," Airy giggled.

Luckily the ground was damp from a recent rain, the grass we walked across lush and soft. Otherwise our bare feet would not have survived the trek across the hills to the copse of trees to stay safe until morning. The warm night felt like velvet on my exposed skin, the moon showing our way. I felt an overwhelming sense of relief at being out of that horrible place.

Once we reached the woods and found a soft spot of leaves to make a nest I convinced Airy to take off her robe to use for our bed. Her pale skin gleamed-- blue in the light cast by the moon, her eyes like pools of darkness. "Gods Airy. I'm glad we're out of Canhavu." She allowed me to kiss her, relaxing against me. Her skin was soft and warm, her breath sweet. "I love you," I whispered, my lips close to her ear.

"I know," she whispered back. I ignored the blatant attempt to annoy me as we came together, giving myself over to her and our mutual pleasure. We fell asleep wrapped tightly together.

The sun was low on the horizon, the dawn sky streaked with gray and mauve when we hiked toward the group of teepees in the distance. The grass was filled with dew, the animals we'd seen the night before nowhere in sight. Peace entered my chest as I took in the streak of silver in the distance that indicated a stream or river, the sound of quail and call of swallows as they scooped bugs out of the air. Our meager breakfast of cheese and apples had used up the rest of our stores. I had a craving for bacon and eggs, my stomach rumbling as we walked.

We were within a quarter mile of the camp when the first cry went up that we'd been seen. It was only a few minutes later that we were surrounded with men dressed in loincloths, feathers in their dark hair. I tried to communicate with them but it was impossible, their expressions hostile as they took in our white skin. They tied our hands and led us back to their camp, leaving us by the community fire, presumably to wait for a higher authority. I had no idea by their dress what tribe they were. Considering the design of the teepees, and where we seemed to be, my best guess was Sioux.

The Lakota Sioux and the Cheyenne had fought in what was known as the Black Hills War when the government discovered gold there. It led to what was known as Custer's last stand when the Indians prevailed. But it didn't stop the government from prevailing in the end, and forcing them onto reservations. I wondered where we were and what year it was.

"Why did I listen to you?" Airy whispered. "The trees told me it was dangerous here. And now I can't get hold of my ring or your hand."

"We don't know if it's dangerous or not, Airy. This is what any self-respecting early tribe would do with people wandering around—especially ones different from themselves."

"We don't speak their language, we—" Her sentence was cut off when an Indian probably in his forties emerged from a teepee covered in buffalo hides and approached us. His dark hair hung on either side of his face in thick braids, his skin brown from the sun as well as his heritage. He wore no shirt over his broad chest, a loincloth and deerskin leggings decorated with beads covering his lower body. He untied us.

"Where you come?" he asked in broken English.

"We come from the future," I answered honestly. I pointed to Airy's hand and the ring. "This ring is magic and we use it to travel."

He stared at the ring and gestured for her to take it off, which she did after casting a worried look at me. He turned it over in his hands, examining the stone before handing it back. "I know this," he said.

Airy raised her eyebrows, her questioning gaze meeting mine.

"We landed in the woods back there," I continued, pointing. "We came from another place that is in the future. It is why I wear no clothes."

"This future place is warm?"

I laughed. "No. It's a long story."

"I would like to hear."

I spent the next forty-five minutes explaining where we'd been, describing the city and Mr. Sand and what he intended for us.

"Good you leave," he finally said. "Not good place."

"No, it isn't."

"Come smoke pipe and then eat."

I turned to help Airy up but the elder shook his head. I heard Airy say *that figures* in my head as I followed him into the teepee. But I knew that women were highly respected in Native cultures, and just didn't participate in smoking the pipe with the men. From what I'd read, women were thought to have more connection to the spirit world and made better healers than the men. Their ability to give birth and their monthly bleeding connected them to mother earth and the cycles of the moon in a special way—visions were expected from them during that time, and the elders listened to what they had to say.

Inside the air was smoky and pungent. Several elders and two younger braves sat around the fire where sage burned on a low grate, the smoke escaping from the hole at the top of the teepee. I joined them in the circle and took in smoke as we passed the pipe, my eyes lowered and watering. Our host told me we smoked Cansasa, 'from the bark of the tree that grows by the river'. "It is filled with Great Spirit and will come into each of us and we will understand all difference."

I didn't know what we were smoking, but I began to hallucinate, imagining a native woman dressed in white deerskin floating in the air above us, her sweet voice singing words I couldn't understand. I saw a hawk land on her shoulder, it's golden eye focused on me. *It is far you have come and farther still to go back. Beware what lies between*, I heard it say. I drifted after that, listening to a chant someone was singing, the rhythmic words and cadence putting me into a stupor.

Sometime later the pipe was laid aside and the man who spoke English began to speak in his own language, and oddly, I could understand. "The Great Spirit has brought these travelers," he said. "They have come to warn us about the future. Oh Great Spirit, hear our voice and make us understand the white man's ways. They come as the heavy rains come, without being summoned, and pour down on us, washing away what we are and what we will become."

Tears formed in my eyes as he continued because I knew that every word he spoke was true. When the ceremony was over and everyone else had left the teepee I asked, "Is the white man close? Have you fought with them?"

His eyes went dark with pain. "The white man has killed many of our people. We move and move again but he follows with the beasts of iron. There are too many."

If trains were traveling across the country we were in the mid-eighteen hundreds or later. In eighteen fifty-one congress would pass the Indian appropriation act and the first reservation would be created.

Airy was sitting with several young women when I emerged from the tent. They had dressed her in deerskin and braided her hair. She took in my nakedness and had to suppress a giggle. "Has anyone mentioned your lack of clothing?"

"No, Airy. I don't think they care."

She motioned me close. "Come have some of this meat. It's been smoked. I think it's venison."

I sat next to her, keeping an eye out for our host and the other men who milled about. The younger ones seemed uncomfortable with us being there; I could feel it like a prickling on my skin. I watched them head off to find the ponies and then ride out, bows and arrows on their backs. "They hunt," our host said, sitting next to me. "They trust no white man."

"I don't blame them," I responded, watching them gallop across the grassland on their pinto ponies.

"What will happen?" he asked, his savvy gaze on mine.

He was asking about the future. I looked away. "Eventually all your people will live on reservations," I told him. "The whites will be in charge."

"Is what I've seen in vision—many dead."

"I'm sorry."

"It is not for you to be sorry."

"I wish I could change things—help you have a different outcome."

He shook his head and bent to take a piece of meat. "You leave when sun is high," he said, "before braves come back from hunt."

"They want us to go?" Airy whispered.

"If we stay the younger men could kill us, Airy. They don't like us being here."

"I cannot stop," he said. "It is our way now."

"I wanted to stay here and find out more about the culture," Airy said as I pulled her to her feet.

"They don't like the white man. We're lucky he was here. Without him we could have been scalped." I thought for a minute. "Airy, why don't we find the town and see what's going on—it will give us more information about this place and maybe we can figure out some way to help the tribe."

"Sounds good, but where is the town? How do we find it?"

Our host pointed. "Is where sun rises--close to mountain."

I suddenly had a thought, turning to Airy. "Can we take these people back in time?"

She glanced at me, her head cocked as though listening. "Maybe. They would all have to be holding hands."

I turned back to him. "Would your people let us take you to a safer time? It would be here, just a hundred years earlier."

"Buffalo still here?"

Were there buffalo in the seventeen hundreds? There must have been. I nodded.

"Young won't like," he said. "They want fight and think fight will save. They not listen to vision."

"You had a vision about us?" Airy asked.

He nodded. "Two travelers from future." He pointed. "You."

"And did we take you to another time?"

He shook his head. "All I see is travelers."

"I think we should go to town first before we take you back," I said, glancing at him.

He nodded his agreement. "Go town and talk. Come back and tell what they say. We have traded with them, thought friends, but if what you say is true, there will no longer be peace."

Airy pointed to my body. "Do you have something for Fehin to wear? I doubt the settlers will be happy to see a naked man arrive in town."

When we left I was wearing deerskin leggings, a necklace of shell beads around my neck for luck. "Come back when sun rise again," he said, gesturing for us to follow him. He grabbed two grazing black and white ponies by the mane and quickly slipped knotted pieces of leather over their noses.

I vaulted onto the pony's back as I'd seen the braves do, but Airy was less sure about how to get on board. Finally he gave her a leg up. "Good ponies—bring back."

"We will," I promised, hoping something wouldn't happen to prevent us from doing so.

Our trip to town was made to the sound of Airy's chattering, her voice lifting and swelling on the soft breeze that followed us.

"…I haven't ridden since I was in Otherworld. I love it! And these ponies are the perfect size….I'm so glad we're out of that other place and we got to meet the tribe…what do you think town will be like? I wonder what year this is---gods, it's so beautiful here, isn't it?"

I barely heard her, consumed with what year it was and where we were. I hoped to hell we weren't anywhere near Wounded Knee where the massacre of several tribes happened at the hands of American soldiers. Spotted Elk had been the leader, his half-brother was Sitting Bull, and his nephew was Crazy Horse, another incredible warrior and leader.

I wasn't sure why it disturbed me so much, since the battles had already happened, but being here felt very different from reading about it in a dry history book that painted a glowing picture of the settlers and the horror of what they had to go through at the hands of the 'savages'. The white man had come into another man's land where they'd lived for thousands of years, and claimed it--in the name of what? If there hadn't been so many whites, the massacres would never have taken place and the Indians would rule this part of the world. I wished I could rewrite history. If I could, the world would have been more in touch with nature and less involved with making money. Money drove everything now and nature was left to fend for itself.

"It's just up ahead," I heard Airy say, looking toward where she gestured. I could see dust rising from a cluster of wooden buildings, the sound of gunshots reaching my ears.

"What the hell?" I muttered.

"Probably a gunfight in town or just some drunk yahoo letting off steam," Airy said, glancing at me calmly.

Since when did she get so pragmatic? "I suggest caution," I said, pulling back on the piece of rawhide in my hands. "We're dressed like Indians and if they see that first, and not the color of our skin, we could be in trouble."

We entered the small settlement on the dusty road at what seemed like the less populated end of town. Once we saw the hitching post that ran along one side of the street we slid off and tied the ponies. I watched Airy unbraid her hair, fluffing it out with her fingers.

"What Indian has hair like mine?" she said, chuckling.

"True enough."

Further up the road we saw a woman dressed in calico hurry across the street carrying a basket. She disappeared through a doorway. A man came out of a building closer to us, his gaze scanning both ways before hurrying across and into another building. There seemed to be some nervousness due to whatever was going on at the other end of the main street. We made our way carefully along the wooden walkway until we came to the post office.

"Let's see if they have a paper," Airy said, opening the wooden door with the two panes of smoky glass set into the top half.

Inside it smelled like cigar smoke and sweat, the floor filthy and covered in dust. I saw a printing press along the back wall, reams of paper next to it. "Do you have a newspaper?" I asked, moving toward the desk.

The man was narrow-eyed and skinny, his boots up on the desk, his hat low over his eyes. He jerked when I spoke and sat up, his boots hitting the wooden floor with a thump. "Who in blazes are you two?" he asked, his surprised gaze going from me to Airy.

"We're traveling from the east and thought these costumes might help us stay out of Indian hands," Airy said, smiling brightly.

"Well, isn't that a strange turn of events," the man said, cocking his hat back. "Never heard of anyone doing that before. What can I do you for?"

"A newspaper," I repeated, glancing around. "We need to see what's happening."

He ignored me, rooting around on his desk. "Here you go, little lady." He held out what looked like a pamphlet. "Not too many people here in Chisholm Springs. News is slow to get here, and there's not much of interest in these parts to write about, other than the occasional Indian uprising. They'll all be on reservations soon. The government has declared the savages a detriment to progress."

I heard the train whistle in the distance. "But you have a train," I said. "What line is it?"

"Kansas Pacific line. How did you two get here if not on the train? Haven't had any wagon trains coming through here for a while."

"We rode from Kansas. It's been a long trip. Any place we can get cleaned up?"

"The saloon has a bathtub, but he charges a goodly amount. You can use the trough around back if you don't mind a little horse spittle." He laughed. "But I'd take care—Jesse James and Belle Starr just arrived and there's plenty of uproar because of it."

My mouth opened in surprise. "How did they end up here?"

He shrugged. "Train came through and they're on the way to somewhere. Guess they wanted to kick up their heels a bit in a place where the law doesn't much exist."

I stared at the August, 1868 date, noticing the headline that read: **All Tribes to be put on reservations!** I held it out to Airy who perused the article, looking bleakly up at me once she was finished. "I think our plan is a good one."

"What plan is that?" the man behind the desk asked.

"We want to wet our whistle at the saloon and then take a bath," I answered, motioning for Airy to come along as I opened the door.

"Hey! That paper doesn't come free!" the guy shouted.

I threw it back at him. "Not enough here to interest me," I said.

Airy and I hurried away, hoping he wouldn't come after us. In the distance I could hear shouting, the sound of a gun being fired. Some idiot had decided to tangle with the outlaws. When Airy headed toward the chaos I grabbed her arm. "Where are you going?"

"I want to see the outlaws and what's happening."

I shook my head and followed her, wondering if I'd regret it.

The saloon loomed into view, the porch in front of it covered in men dressed in cowboy boots and dusty long coats, guns hanging from their belts. In the middle of the street I saw a very pregnant woman with a round face standing next to a dark-haired man. He had a mustache and his face was angular, his chin sharp. Someone shouted, "What do you say, Jesse? Want to try your hand with me?"

A drunken man swaggered off the porch, his hand on his gun. In the street the woman whispered something in the gunslinger's ear and headed away, her hand on her enormous belly. I watched her join a man on the other side of the street, the two of them disappearing through a doorway.

It was only a minute later that the two faced off. And a moment after that the drunk lay on his back in the dust, the gunshots still reverberating in my ears. The crowd dispersed, no one else coming forward to tangle with Jesse James.

"Who was that woman? Was it Belle Starr? How could she expose herself like that when she's about to give birth?"

"I think it was Belle. I read somewhere that she had a baby around this time. Pretty foolhardy."

I've had enough of this town," Airy said, glancing at me. "I don't want to get shot. I say we go get the ponies and ride back. We can move the tribe sooner rather than later. Who knows when the authorities will arrive and begin rounding them up?"

"I think it was a bit more complicated than that," I answered. "The Indians didn't go quietly, Airy. It was a major bloodbath that took years."

"I've read all about it, Fehin. It makes me ashamed to be white."

I grimaced and took her arm, heading away from the dead man with the hole in his chest who nobody seemed concerned about. We rode out of town, pushing the sturdy ponies into a canter to escape the screams and shouting that had begun again--some other nitwit deciding to commit suicide by Jesse James?

Once we'd left the road behind and headed into the grassy hills we slowed the horses, turning to see men on the road riding hard, the dust swirling around them as they galloped toward Chisholm Springs. More outlaws, or was this the law coming to arrest them?

"If I didn't know better I'd be afraid they were after us," Airy said, squinting into the distance.

"I know what you mean. As soon as we relocate the tribe let's get the heck out of here."

It took several hours of discussion before the tribe decided who was going and who was staying. Many of the younger braves had decided to remain, their angry stares making me nervous as they rounded up their wives and children. But our man held up his hand and said a few words that calmed them down. When I told him about the Black Hills War, and the Cheyenne, his eyes went dark.

"Cheyenne friend. Live not far." He pointed in an easterly direction.

"There could be other tribes in the past, other problems," I warned him. "We can make it even earlier if you like."

"When Spanish here?"

How did he know about the Spanish? "They were here in the sixteen hundreds. Does that seem a better time?"

He shook his head no. "First choice best," he said, his fist on his heart. "Killed by tribe better than reservation. I have seen future when ghost dance bring soldiers."

He knew about the ghost dance? The movement wouldn't start until the 1890's. And he was right. Many Indians were killed at Wounded Knee because of it. I wondered who this man was.

The Indians who decided to make the trip held hands, the line of men, women and children stretching at least a quarter mile. Some held ponies too and I wondered if the animals would be a problem. Once everyone was assembled our host held up his hand to signal Airy to begin. "Take us to this exact spot in 1751," she whispered, rubbing her ring.

The rift opened, revealing a sky dark with storm clouds, the landscape bleak. Possibly it was winter. Our host was at the head of the line, his interested gaze going into the gap. "Time of cold," he said. And then Airy went ahead and everyone followed. Once they were all through, the rift closed behind us. I watched the ponies gallop away as though spooked by what had just happened. Our host looked at me, his eyes bright. "Is good," he said. "Many buffalo."

I looked where he pointed noticing the large herds that roamed across the snowy hills. A sharp wind came up and I shivered, suddenly very aware of my naked chest. "You don't have your buffalo hides or teepees," I said, worried.

"We live in woods until build. Go now."

"I wish you well," I said, holding out my hand.

He took hold of my arm. "Spotted Elk remember. It will be written." His deep eyes met mine, a smile pulling at the corners of his wide mouth.

He was Spotted Elk? We were definitely changing history. Behind me Airy was already rubbing her ring. Maybe if we found Wovoka, the Paiute spiritual leader who developed the ghost dance, we could stop Wounded Knee from happening. "Do you know Wovoka?" I asked him. "If I found him maybe I—"

He shook his head. "It is written and will come to pass," he said. "I have seen in vision. Go!" he said again, glancing toward Airy.

"But what about your part? What about--"

But he turned away, his focus on where they were. Airy grinned, watching me shiver. "I guess we'd better go."

She always seemed to get a kick out of my discomfort. I nodded my agreement despite not looking forward to appearing in the middle of Milltown dressed in deerskin leggings. At least I could find regular clothes there. Airy grabbed my hand, and the last thing I saw was Spotted Elk's nod of confidence as we whirled away into the ether.

Instead of Milltown, we landed in the middle of a village filled with rustic huts. Children were everywhere, no adults to be seen. They fought in the thick mud in the street, their sharp cries making the hair at the back of my neck stand up. Their faces were streaked with the stuff, the ragged clothing as well. It was then I noticed the knives carved out of wood and sharpened to points. I watched one kid around ten year's old plunge one of these into another, saw the other boy go down and knew that he was dead. It reminded me of the book my mother had given me when I was younger called, 'Lord of the Flies'. Where were the adults? When one of them noticed us he signaled several others. They were advancing on us when

Airy yelled, "Wrong timeline!" and grabbed my hand. We whirled away.

I hit my head when we landed, letting out a roar of pain. We were in the middle of Milltown on a sidewalk, the sound of traffic rolling by, horns honking and the general buzz and din of a medium sized city. I saw the utter shock on faces as people moved past, especially when I stood up and realized that the leggings had disintegrated into dust around my feet. Airy wasn't much better in her deerskin dress that had done the same. I heard my shell beads plunk onto the pavement and bent to scoop them up. The string that held them had dissolved as well.

She stared at me, eyes wide in her pale face. "I'm naked," she whispered.

"We better get off the street before we're arrested," I whispered back. I grabbed her hand and hurried toward an alley between two buildings, but a second later I saw a cop coming toward us.

"What in god's name are you two up to? " he asked, cuffing us. A minute later he perp-marched us out of the alley to his waiting patrol car.

"I've got two naked kids here," I heard him say into his hand-held device after we were deposited in back of the squad car. "I'm bringing 'em in."

"You better get in touch with Carla," I whispered in Airy's ear. "She's the only person who can help." Carla knew my mother, and had taken us in shortly after we arrived in Milltown for college. She supported us during all the weird stuff that had happened over the past two years, even giving us her car. I hated the thought of asking her for help again, but I couldn't think of anyone else.

Airy glanced at me, her gaze scanning across my naked and shivering body. She giggled.

"Shut it, you two," the cop said. "There's nothing funny about indecent exposure."

At the station after the cop had removed our cuffs and another cop had brought us each a blanket, Airy called Carla. A few minutes later she turned to me with a frown. "The number is not in service."

I stared, surprised. "Do you think she moved?"

Airy shrugged. "Did you notice how different Milltown is? The market on the corner is gone and I didn't see the college." She turned to the man behind the desk. "What year is it?"

He frowned. "What kind of question is that? I think the two of you are destined for the psych ward."

Airy shook her head. "Judging from the warm weather it has to be summer. Carla couldn't have moved this quickly."

"So what does it mean?"

"It either means we've changed things with our time-traveling, or that we're in a parallel reality."

"Like string theory—an alternate reality?"

"I don't know much about the theory, but it's one way to explain..."

We stopped talking when a cop came toward us holding a clipboard. "I need names and addresses, please," he said, handing us each a clipboard. "Also the names of your parents or others who can vouch for you."

"What happened to Milltown College?" Airy asked, taking the clipboard.

The cop looked confused. "We don't have a college here. And this town is called Grayson." He turned and walked away.

I glanced at Airy. "I don't much like this," I whispered. "We don't know anyone here and we don't have addresses." I glanced at her ring.

"You want me to take us to some other place? How? I asked to go to Milltown and here we are."

"This is Grayson."

At that moment another cop headed our way and the look on his face was none too friendly. "If we get separated we're shit out of luck," I hissed, taking hold of her hand.

Her eyes met mine and I saw her move the stone to face inward before she closed her palm. "Milltown with Carla!" she shouted. I saw the startled expression on the cop's face before we entered the swirl of darkness.

It was barely a second before we were somewhere else, and this somewhere else looked a lot like the Milltown we'd just left. Except for one glaring difference. There were no cars, no trees and only a few people walking though a city of deserted buildings and rubble. The police station was still where it had been, but the door hung wide and leaves and detritus blew in and out as the wind shifted. "What the hell?"

Airy shrugged. "I tried, you heard me."

"Maybe Carla is here somewhere. Let's go find out."

"Not before we find some clothes, Fehin. It's cold here and all we have is these crappy blankets." She pulled the blanket tight around her body and led the way across the empty square and then past several homeless huddled along the street and a few tough looking punks who I didn't want to tangle with. All of them had blankets similar to ours wrapped around their shoulders. Fifteen minutes later we arrived at the apartment where Carla lived, but I knew as soon as I saw the building that she wasn't there. "This was a bust," I muttered, staring at the broken steps, the door hanging crookedly on one hinge, the shattered windows and glass shards that littered the uneven sidewalk.

"I'm very sorry," Airy said, near to tears.

"I'm not blaming you. I heard what you said, and unless you were thinking something very different there's no reason why we ended up here."

She looked up, her eyes watery. "I did—I did think something different."

"What?"

"I was thinking about dystopian futures and what might happen if past and future collided. I was wishing we could have changed the outcome of the country instead of only relocating the tribe. You know how your mind does this stuff."

"I know how *your* mind does this stuff—you have no control over your thoughts at all, do you?"

"That's not fair!"

I pressed my lips together and raised my eyebrows. "Present circumstances kind of prove it, Airy."

"I said I was sorry!" she shouted.

I headed for the steps, avoiding the glass as I walked up.

"Where are you going?"

"I'm wondering if any of my clothes got left behind," I said, entering the dark and dingy front room.

"You were probably never here!" she yelled. I heard her crying as I placed my shell beads down on top of the dresser in what had once been our bedroom. I pulled out the drawers that had held my clothes, gratified to find a pair of jeans and a T-shirt. I pulled them on and looked around for my boots, not surprised to find them in the closet. I grabbed the army fatigue jacket I'd been wearing when I came back after...I stopped my thoughts, not wanting to go down that particular memory lane. It had been a very hard time for both of us.

I turned as Airy appeared in the doorway. "Did you--?" She stared at me, her question cut short. A second later she was pawing through her section of the room, coming up with a pair of ripped jeans and a plaid button-up shirt. "I guess this is better than the blanket," she said, letting it drop.

When it fell to the floor I stared at her naked body, heat rising from my toes into my neck and face. I moved toward her, grabbing her arm just as she was stepping into her jeans. "Can we take a moment, Airy? I need to connect."

She turned, her eyebrows rising as she registered the expression on my face. "Again? We just did that."

I felt a blush move into my face. I shrugged and smirked. "That seems like a lifetime ago. What better place than the room where we first had sex?"

She glanced at the bed. "Well, I…"

I dragged her by the hand, hopping on one leg to get my jeans off. We fell on the bed together and I kissed her. "This will help, I promise," I murmured, my fingers tracing across her soft skin.

"Not sure what it will help with, but it's a nice diversion," she muttered, her arms going around my neck.

CHAPTER FIVE
AIRY

When Fehin kissed me I forgot all about our problems, focusing instead on the feel of his skin against mine, and how good we were together. My mind went to the first time, here in this room, after he'd been gone nearly a year. And then I forgot even that.

Later, when we lay tangled together, I looked up at him. "I do love you, you know."

"I love you too," he said, sliding his leg across mine. "I have a suggestion regarding the stone."

I pushed myself up on one elbow. "What?"

"You need to learn to meditate, Airy, to clear you mind before you ask it to take us somewhere."

I frowned at him and turned away. The stone was mine to command, not his. "I did clear my mind, I just..."

"No, you didn't. If you had we wouldn't be here and we might not have traveled to that god-awful place in the future.

You have to concentrate like you did when you sent that tribe back one hundred years."

I sat up and reached for my shirt. "You don't know for sure Mr. Sand was in the future. And what about the Indians—that was kind of cool. They even took some of the ponies along."

"Yes, you did good with the tribe. Stop being defensive and think about this. We need to find our way back to the right Milltown, don't we? To do that you have to control your thoughts."

"Okay, master, what do you suggest?"

"Sit quietly here on the bed while I look around the kitchen and see if there's any food or tea, or if the stove works."

"Sit here—and what?"

"Breathe, Airy. Just pay attention to your breath."

I watched him pull on his jeans and head into the other room, my mind going to what we'd just done and how good it felt. And then I closed my eyes and listened to the breath coming in and out, in and out, in and out...

"Airy!"

I opened my eyes and pushed myself up to sitting. "I guess I fell asleep."

Fehin frowned and shook his head. He handed me a cup of tea and plunked down an unopened bag of popcorn. "There isn't much here. I'm surprised the place hasn't been cleaned out by the homeless."

"We could squat here."

"For what purpose?"

I shrugged and took a sip. "I don't know. It just feels like home, that's all."

"What are we doing, anyway?" he asked, ripping open the bag of popcorn. "Are we experimenting with time travel, trying to change something in the past to help the future, or just attempting to have a good time?"

"My first idea was to have fun, but now…" I stared at the wall, noticing that it was covered in mold. "After what happened to us I want to make sure the world goes in the right direction." I rose and found my jeans and shirt, pulling them on.

Fehin stuffed a handful of popcorn in his mouth. "Tall order. Do you think this place is the result of the world going in the wrong direction or string theory?"

"How am I supposed to know?"

Fehin made a derisive sound in the back of his throat. "Just an opinion, Airy; I'm not asking you to figure out the universe and everything in it."

"If I had to guess I'd say we're in another dimension—I think there's supposed to be ten of them."

"The ten dimensions don't refer to ten parallel universes. The fourth dimension is time and the fifth and sixth refers to other possible worlds. Seven is about other worlds having different initial conditions, so whatever evolved there would not match up with our known universe. The eighth is a plane of infinite possible worlds each with different start conditions. Ninth is *all* possible worlds beginning with all possible start conditions and the law of physics. Ten is infinite possibilities."

I stared at him in surprise. "I didn't know you'd studied physics."

He shrugged. "I took half a semester before I dropped out of college."

"The eighth and ninth sound very similar, and ten—well, ten is terrifying. Are we in ten?"

"It's all theoretical, Airy. I have no idea where we are, only that there's a lot more out there than what we know. As to your ring—you need to be way more specific about where you want to go."

"Okay, Mr. Guru who knows all about dimensions, you come up with it." I pulled the moonstone off my finger and handed it to him.

Fehin grabbed hold of me, the ring clutched in his other hand as he stared into space. "Take us to the Milltown where we went to college," he said. When nothing happened he held the ring out. "Guess it only works for you."

I placed it in my palm, peering at the opaque rose-gray stone. "I wish I knew why I feel so strongly about everything bad that's happening. It's like I've lived before in some parallel world where things were good."

"You mean like Otherworld?"

"Well, yes, that, but—humans aren't evolving, Fehin, we're going backward." I gazed at him. "It's like money has become the driving force and everything good is being churned under. I'd like to see if something happened in the past to put us on such a destructive path." A moment later I felt the familiar sensation of time distortion, watching Fehin's expression of shock as I disappeared from view. "No!" I shouted, but it was too late. I was already spinning into the dark.

CHAPTER SIX
FEHIN

I stared at the spot on the bed where Airy had been a moment before. The familiar plaid comforter was scrunched and wrinkled, and when I placed my palm there it was still warm. What in hell did she say to have this happen? And more importantly, how would we find each other again? This entire plan was a screwed up mess. I headed into the other room, hoping to hear Airy's voice as she reappeared, but as I searched through cabinets for something more nutritious to eat there was only the sound of the wind whistling through the broken windows.

I was eating beans out of a can when Gunnar appeared, the druid's eyebrows knitted together in a frown of irritation. "What in hell are you up to?" he asked.

Gunnar and I had had several disagreements in the past and I knew he had little fondness for me. "What are you talking about?"

The druid's eyes narrowed. "You know exactly what I'm talking about, Fehin. You and Airy are meddling with time." He scanned the room. "Where is she?"

"You're the all-seeing time traveler—don't you know?"

"Don't push me, boy. I have no time for this."

I laughed. "I'm no longer a boy, Gunnar, and I thought time was your stock and trade. How can you have no time?"

He shook his head, exasperated. "I should never have brought you into the past."

"You *helped* bring me into the past, Gunnar. And according to you it was my destiny. I'm sure I would have made it here without you. Airy and I were supposed to meet."

"Actually, that is not true. I was part of your destiny, the one tasked with getting you to where you were supposed to be. Do you have any idea what you've done?"

"What specifically are you talking about?"

"I'm talking about moving a Native American tribe over one hundred years into the past. Do either of you have a brain in your head? Those people are related to the people who lived then—their lineage will be completely destroyed by this one act of stupidity." He looked around again. "So where is Airy?"

"She disappeared about a half hour ago. If I could remember exactly what she said to have the ring take her away I'd tell you, but all I can remember is her asking questions about why the world is the way it is."

Gunnar stared into the distance. "I can't see her." He turned to me. "That means she's in another dimension. Were you discussing dimensions?"

I nodded and threw the empty can into the trash. "She said something about humans not evolving and then she was gone."

"I won't be able to find her if she's where I think she is."

"And where is that?"

"With the gods, Fehin. They are the keepers of the universe and live in a separate dimension. They are the only ones who could answer a question like that. And since I have no sense of her anywhere else I fear that's where she's gone."

His use of the word fear sent a shiver down my back. "Can we travel there and get her back?"

Gunnar shook his head. "It is off limits. And it's not really a place; it's more like a mind state. She will have a hard time negotiating the intricacies since she will not be corporeal."

"What should I do?"

"Wait and hope like hell she finds her way back."

"We got here by accident, Gunnar. I'm not sure if it's Grayson or Milltown."

"Don't you think I know that? How do you think I found you?"

"I don't know. How do you track?"

"I follow your energy signatures. It led me here. You better hope to hell she comes back, because this particular place you're in is about to undergo a rather nasty transformation."

"I don't know how she could find it again." I shook my head, exasperated. "She has no control of that damn ring—we almost ended up as prey in one of our forays into the time/space continuum."

Gunnar scoffed. "I was about to bail you out of there when Airy did it for me. You shouldn't be complaining about Airy, Fehin. Without her you're stuck here."

"Glad to know you're always looking out for us. If this place is about to get weird, how about you take me with you?"

"I've been instructed to look out for Airy, not you."

"Why do you hate me so much?"

"Because you—" He stopped himself and stared into space.

"Because I have powers that you don't? Or is it because I got rid of my brother, who would have destroyed the world? Come on, Gunnar, admit it--you're jealous of me." The druid swallowed, a sure sign I'd hit a nerve. "Is it my destiny to die here in some facsimile of Milltown?"

He shook his head. "And your mother will not be happy with me if I leave you here," he muttered. "This place is about to be overrun by something that you and Airy created."

"Created? How?"

"I should have said 'allowed in'. Yours and Airy's little games have caused gaps in time and rips that need to be repaired, not to mention what you did with the Sioux tribe. But without her, there is no way to fix anything."

I frowned at him. "You travel all over the place in time— why don't your trips need to be repaired?"

The druid peered at me, gray brows furrowed over dark eyes. "Because I know what I'm doing."

I scoffed at that. "Can you tell me what's coming? I might prefer taking my chances here."

"I don't know what form it will take—could be humans from another time who are bent on war, or it could be beings that only exist in some other reality. All I can tell you is that it's destined to destroy this town and everything in it. And when they get finished here the chaos will move on."

"But this isn't even Milltown, is it? What year are we in?"

"The year has little bearing since it's another possible reality. But that doesn't make what you two did any better. Airy has to repair the tears or the entire planet is doomed."

"But if this is another reality why can't we just go back to the one where Airy and I went to school? They can't get from here to there, can they?"

"You don't get it, Fehin. You've created a rift in time in all dimensions. I will do what I can, but if we don't find Airy the situation will become untenable."

I crossed my arms over my chest feeling a deep chill. "I want to stay here in case she comes back. But I have the feeling that she'd be more likely to end up in the real Milltown. She has to say the month and the year—that's it, isn't it?"

Gunnar nodded. "Not sure why you two idiots didn't figure that out sooner. I can take you to the proper Milltown, if that's what you want. At least it will buy you some time."

I sighed, looking around the dingy house, the smell of mold and the spider webs in every corner. "Okay. But how can I find Airy?"

"You can't. That's what I've been trying to tell you. She's lost to us unless she finds her way to you. And unless she has her wits about her, the place of the gods will seduce her."

I let out a gasp. "You mean she won't want to leave?"

Gunnar's brows knitted into a frown of worry. "That's what I mean."

"Crap. Don't you know anyway we can—?"

He shook his head and grabbed my arm and a second later we were in the ether, wind moving by at an accelerating speed until we landed in the very same room. This time sunlight was streaming through the unbroken and open windows and our friend and surrogate mother, Carla, was standing in the kitchen.

Her brown eyes lit up when she saw me. "Fehin! I thought you and Airy were on walkabout!" She glanced at Gunnar. "And good to see you again. Where is Airy?"

"She accidentally took herself into another time-line, and—"

"And she may be in trouble," Gunnar finished for me.

"Trouble—how?"

"She's with the gods, I guess—the ones who made the universe?" I looked to the druid for corroboration.

"The Annunaki—the immortal gods who are said to have created the universe," Carla said. "They came from the planet Nibiru."

"Yes," Gunnar agreed.

"And this planet has been seen by astronomers, but NASA refuses to acknowledge its existence," I said, remembering the readings I'd done outside of class.

"That is also correct," Gunnar said.

"That's where she is?" I asked.

Gunnar didn't shake his head yes or no, his gaze going to Carla. "What do you know of the Annunaki?"

"That they're a myth? I heard two accounts—one that they were gods who bred with humans and created what we are today, the other that they were aliens from another planet that wanted to enslave us. They were also known as the Watchers in the Bible, responsible for God's creation until they rebelled and bred with human women. Don't tell me any of this is true."

"Not at its basis, no. God did not create them, nor did they rebel against God. They are beings of light, avatars, just as the fallen angel, Lucifer, who continues to inform us through our dreams, intuition and higher knowing. I am quite certain Airy is with them."

"And they will make sure she comes back where she belongs," Carla said, glancing at me.

Gunnar looked down.

"Gunnar says that being with them is seductive. Airy may choose to stay."

Carla scoffed. "That girl loves you, Fehin. She won't choose to remain somewhere knowing she'll never see you again."

"Let's hope her love is strong enough to bring her back," Gunnar said, frowning at me.

Carla glanced from me to Gunnar. "What do we do?"

"We hope we see her again before what she started rips through the fabric of time and destroys our world," the druid replied.

Carla's eyes went wide. "What?"

But Gunnar didn't answer, and a second later he disappeared as neatly as he'd appeared.

"What's going on, Fehin?"

"You know as much as I do. Apparently Airy and I have created some sort of time anomaly or rip or something. If she doesn't fix it, beings from other time lines will come into the present and wreak havoc, or at least that's what Gunnar says."

"And you trust him?"

I shrugged. "We don't get along, but I've never known him to outright lie unless he wants something."

"What might he want?"

"I can't think of anything. And I know he loves Airy. If he could find her he would. I just hope she isn't caught up in whatever ethereal nonsense the gods are feeding her."

"In other words you believe in these gods and that she's in some other dimension?"

I nodded and pulled a chair out. "Do you have a beer handy?"

She grimaced. "I think something stronger is in order," she said, reaching for the bottle of brandy on the counter.

I didn't argue.

CHAPTER SEVEN

AIRY

I couldn't figure out where I was. It felt like a cushion of air was holding me up, and when I tried to see my hand, or any part of my body, there was nothing there but a foggy haze. I heard a voice in my head calling to me in dulcet tones. "Yes?" I answered.

"You want to know where it all started," the voice said.

The male voice reminded me of some movie I'd seen. "I wanted to see if I could help," I answered.

"It needs to fix itself, Airy. Humans are responsible for the problems they create and must find their way out. If you stay here with us you will see what I mean. Come closer."

"I don't think my body is actually here," I answered, trying to move my feet. A second later the clouds that seemed to hem me in, cleared. I was standing on alabaster steps and before me was the most beautiful being I'd ever seen. If angels existed he was one, golden hair to his shoulders, white robes hanging in graceful folds to the sandals on his exquisite feet. His eyes were a shade between pale green and silver, the iris's liquid and changing as he gazed on me from a few steps above. The building behind him was gold and white, elegant arches lifting into a cerulean sky filled with billowy white clouds. If heaven existed this must be it.

He smiled. "There you are." He held out his hand and led me to where he stood, his strange eyes never leaving mine. "Come sit and we can talk." He kept hold of my hand and led me to two chairs on the next level that hadn't been there a moment before. He pulled one out and gestured for me to sit. "You have been busy, haven't you? There has been a lot of discussion and consternation among us about what you have done, but we all agree that it will sort itself without our intervention." He turned as a woman dressed in a pale rose toga appeared. He nodded to her and she headed away.

"Now what was I saying? Oh yes. About your question—it is a very complicated issue since there are so many differing possibilities. So many worlds and too many beginnings to fathom, especially for a human brain like yours." The woman appeared with two delicate golden cups, placing them on the table between us. He picked one up and handed it to me. "Drink and then we will continue our conversation."

I did as he asked, savoring the sweet honey-like liquid, feeling it soothe my throat and lighten my mood. "What is this?"

"It is our special drink. It comes from our fruit trees. Come, I have much to show you."

He rose and held out his hand and I took it, following him through a high arched doorway. Golden light followed us, seeming to pulsate, sending a glow into the walls, the floors, the ceiling, and even the air itself. I could feel it on my skin like a warming glow. "Is this heaven?"

He laughed. "No, Airy. This is a dimension untouched by your world. We were originally tasked with watching over your species, but we no longer have that responsibility. You are on your own now."

"So that's why we are no longer evolving? I have always felt that I came from some place where things were…"

"Where things were evolving. You did. The entire human species did, but they have forgotten all of that."

"Why?"

He stopped in a courtyard filled with trees laden with fruit that resembled pears, but instead of the normal green and reddish tones, these were a pearlescent color that shimmered, changing from rose to turquoise to orange. Inside the graceful tree branches tiny colorful birds flitted, their voices lilting. The air was filled with the perfume of the drink I'd just been given. My host turned to me, gesturing to the stone bench. When I sat he sat next to me.

"There is too much fear, which leads to violence," he continued, answering my question. "Emotions of this nature make it impossible to receive messages from the divine source. I am not talking of God; I am talking of the universe where all the answers exist. All it requires is listening. The churches have been instrumental in creating the fear and guilt that your species carry. Each human being is born with this connection to the divine, but as you mature it is obliterated by conditioning—most can no longer hear it. The world you live in has been taken over by this fear-based mentality. Until that is rectified the human race will continue in its downward spiral."

"I thought if I went back far enough I could figure it out and maybe help in some way."

"You are helping by being here with me, with us, Airy. You will see this as time goes by."

"But I have to get back. Fehin—"

"Fehin will be fine. He is now with Carla."

"How did that happen?"

"The druid has intervened."

I let out a sigh of relief. "Gunnar. I'm so glad."

"Now you must go with Marria. Tonight you will meet the rest of us, or at least the ones who are here at this time."

I turned to see the same woman, her pale sage eyes on me. She gave a nod and I followed her across the courtyard and through another archway. She walked down a long hallway made of white stone and turned right into a light-filled room. "This is yours," she said, showing me the enormous bathroom of marble, the canopied bed, and a high antique-looking dresser. She opened wooden doors into an enormous closet, revealing the gossamer dresses hanging there. "These are yours to wear." She pulled out a saffron gown and held it up. "For tonight I suggest this."

When I took it out of her hands she turned to go. "Wait! Where do I go and when?"

"Bathe and dress and I will come for you when the time is right."

I wondered if they'd expected me. It sure seemed that way from all the clothes that appeared to be just my size and the room set up for a guest. I headed into the bathroom and turned on the taps.

It was an hour or more before I heard a soft knock on the door. "Come in." I was dressed and ready, admiring the fabric and the way the color made my green eyes pop.

Marria smiled. "You look beautiful," she said.

"Do you work here?" I asked, hurrying after her.

She laughed. "Oh no. No one works here. We all do our various jobs as they come up. We are not normally in this state."

"This state. Do you mean corporeal?"

"Yes."

"So what are you, usually?"

"It is hard to describe. I suppose light would be one word I might use."

"How did you know to prepare the room—the clothes?"

She turned, her sage eyes meeting mine. "We know when a visitor is arriving."

"But—" My question was cut short as we entered a dining room with an enormous table set with crystal and real silverware. Around it were seated men and women of varying ages, all of them just as beautiful as my host and Marria. I noticed immediately that they were light-skinned with golden hair.

Marria led me to an open seat and pulled out the chair. Once I was seated she moved to another open seat on the far end.

"This is Airy, our guest," my host announced from the head of the table.

"To Airy," everyone said together, raising the crystal goblets.

"Now, Airy, you must tell us how we've done with the meal. It isn't often we have the pleasure of taking food."

A man and a woman arrived from another room carrying platters, which they served around. When it got to me I scooped out a piece of perfectly cooked salmon on a bed of saffron rice. Another platter held asparagus and lightly braised green beans topped with slivered almonds. A silver dish of hot rolls lay on the table, the occupants passing it along. I heard the murmur of conversation--saw only welcoming smiles when my gaze met theirs. I relaxed and ate, murmuring over the deliciousness of the food. It was exceptional.

I fielded questions as I ate and drank, unwilling to reveal too much about myself. It seemed that they already knew, anyway. I got the distinct impression that they expected me to be here for some time, as they talked about foods I might like to try and activities that could keep me from being bored. When Marria walked me back to my room later I asked, "Is my being here a treat for your people?"

"Yes, I suppose it is. We all enjoy the hedonistic pleasures of your species."

"How long do they want me to stay?"

Her eyes widened. "Why, forever, I imagine."

I shook my head. "I can't do that. I have a boyfriend and a life."

"Boyfriend. What does that mean?"

"It means we love each other. He misses me when I'm gone and he worries."

"We have nothing of that sort. We are the watchers and we only get to experience these things vicariously when we are watching over your planet. But we no longer do that."

"You've given up on us."

"There is no more we can do for you." She turned to go.

"How can I fix it?"

"Fix your planet? You cannot. The collective has grown too strong."

"You mean the collective unconscious?"

"It is as it is, Airy. It is out of reach for us and for you."

"But you could if you wanted to."

"Maybe, but it would only happen again. This has been going on for millennia."

"We've come to a good point in our development and then fear has taken over—is that what you mean?"

"A long time ago your planet was run by the females of your species. But the decision was collectively made to give it over to the males for a while. The trouble began with that ill-fated plan. It is time for women to take back the reins, but the violence and greed has grown too strong. It is a lost cause."

After that disturbing statement she walked out the open door and closed it behind her. I sat on the edge of the bed thinking about what she said. These beings were immortal, omnipotent, and yet they would do nothing for us. Anger rose in me. They could stop this downward trend if they wanted to. They had the means to make people understand. I threw the door open and hurried down the hallway, determined to talk with either Marria or my host.

I came upon him in the courtyard of trees. He turned when I rushed in, a concerned look on his handsome face. "What is it, Airy?"

"Why won't you help? You can and you choose not to! This is wrong!"

He smiled sadly. "We are always available for anyone who reaches out to us, Airy. All they need do is ask for our help. But we cannot force ourselves on anyone."

"But they are only misguided, they…"

"And what can we do about it? I ask this question seriously."

"You can imbue them with understanding, send messages to them about their fear, their anger."

"We have tried that and it did not work. In some cases it made things worse. Don't you see? We are not separate—we are part of every human being who is born. All anyone has to do is open their mind."

"Like Jesus?"

"No, not like Jesus. Jesus is a separate being, an avatar as well, but one who led people. He is an influence, not a conduit that exists inside each being."

"And why are all of you white skinned? I find that disturbing."

He laughed. "We appear to you in a form that we think will make you the most comfortable. If you were brown-skinned we would all be brown, Asian, we would be Asian."

I stared at him. "And what is your name?"

"You can call me whatever you like. As a light being I don't need a name. I appeared male to you because of what I know of your relationship with your mother. Perhaps you'd like to call me Lucifer."

He knew about my arguments? "Lucifer was a fallen angel."

He shook his head. "No, Airy, Lucifer was a being of light who arrived before all your religious nonsense began. He was and is an avatar."

"So you blame all this fear and hating on religion?"

"There are many factors that have contributed to your species turning away from the light. Females hold the knowledge of the earth inside them and understand the web that holds it together. But men have subjugated them, rejecting their wisdom. With men in charge your planet suffers."

"And embracing their dark side?"

"There is no dark and light. This is another concept your species has invented, along with the bad being below and the good being above--all man-made beliefs. Everyone has bad and good within them, and some things people consider bad are not bad at all. Every human being makes a choice to turn away from the part of themselves that is connected to the divine. I merely use the term to describe what we are, which is beings of light—tiny pinpricks that are not visible."

"Except now."

"Except now," he echoed, watching me.

"I need to go back—when can I go back?"

"I had hoped you would stay with us for a while." He smiled. "We all enjoy having bodies and what that means— but if you are ready to go we will not force you to stay."

"And how do I figure out where Fehin is?"

"He is with Carla, Airy. When you use the stone concentrate on the two of them together."

I nodded. "Thanks for answering my questions."

"I'm glad you sought me out. Now please rest."

"One more question—is there anything I can do to help the situation on earth?"

His expression turned sad. "I have no advice to give you, only that you need to be careful. There is a very dark time coming."

"You just used the word dark to describe something bad," I said, staring hard at him.

"Yes. It is a figure of speech, I'm afraid, one that has no equivalent. I suppose I could have said bleak, or dangerous. But somehow those words are not as descriptive. I do like language, but I find it oddly annoying at times. There are not enough words for love, for instance."

"English seems to be lacking in some areas."

"Yes. Japanese has fifty words for rain." He patted me on the arm. "Will you leave tomorrow?"

"I don't know. I may have more questions before I go. I'll sleep on it."

When I reached the room I was more confused than ever. It would take more than one lifetime to understand the way the universe worked. How could we have turned away from what we were? It was hard to comprehend. I'd studied Jung and knew about the collective unconscious. The way I thought of it was like a river of fear and confusion that ran around the earth, a river that was hard to avoid falling into. But with resolve people could either pull themselves out or keep free of it. Maybe I did need to meditate after all. Maybe if everyone meditated we'd have less destructive thoughts in the river and come back to our divine roots.

I gazed around the perfect room, the beautiful clothes that hung in the closet, the golden light that filtered in from somewhere. I missed Fehin and all the muddle and chaos of life on earth. I wanted to go home. Had my questions been answered? Not really. But now I realized there were no answers, only more and more questions. It was like what the Buddha said—life is suffering and the only way out is nirvana, the place where suffering disappears. But how many people can reach nirvana?

I climbed onto the high bed and watched the golden light play along the domed ceiling. I saw tiny pinpricks of light behind my eyes as I closed them, sinking into a place of peace. The thought came that if I were to stay here I would be happy always. But how could I live without Fehin in my life?

CHAPTER EIGHT
FEHIN

When shouts rang out I tore down the street away from the fighting. I didn't look back because I knew what I would see—the same thing I'd been seeing for several days. Rough men dressed in archaic and filthy clothes attacking anyone they came upon, beating them with whatever they had at hand, or simply knifing them to death. Blood ran in the streets, the carnage so bad that even the police had no clue what to do. They were dressed in riot gear now, trying to stave off something that couldn't be stopped. I heard screams as tear gas canisters were flung from police vans, the rat-a-tat of guns being fired. The only saving grace was that the people coming through the rift didn't have guns. But I wasn't sure how long it would be before they either discovered them, or people from later times would begin to emerge through the gap in time.

Had Airy become lost in the ether or didn't she know where I was? I hoped to hell she hadn't succumbed to the charms of the gods and decided to stay. She'd been gone over two weeks now. The 'problems', for lack of a better word, had begun a week before—so much for buying some time. If Airy didn't get back to repair the rift soon the place would be overrun. I'd finally convinced Carla to take her daughter, Fan, and drive west. "Hide out in the mountains," I'd told her. She hadn't argued, packing a bag for them both and driving out of town with her foot pressed down on the gas.

The recent newspaper had talked of unrest across the country and around the world. What we'd done was having repercussions I could barely imagine. I thought of the tribe safely in the past, hoping things were going well for them. Spotted Elk had seemed sure of the rightness of it all. He was a visionary, a mystic in his own right.

I saw the National Guard trucks arrive as I was slipping behind the college buildings, hoping to stay out of the line of fire. The college was closed until further notice, all doors locked. There was no place safe.

I headed into the small copse of trees behind the college and tried to contact Airy telepathically. This was where I'd first shown Airy my own magic, conjuring a tiny medieval village in order to help her with her history class. Could I manage this on a larger scale? I certainly had been able to where I lived in the future, but here in the twenty-first century magic was harder to accomplish. Was that because there was a general consensus that it didn't work, or other reasons? I closed my eyes, hoping to hear from her, but there was only the steady cacophony of guns, shrieking and sirens in the distance.

A few minutes later I waved my hands in the familiar patterns saying a few words in the ancient tongue I'd been taught. A second later a soldier wearing armor rose from the leaves and detritus, his eyes vacant. I conjured ten of them and set them marching toward the chaos in the distance.

I followed, maneuvering them with my magic toward the ones coming through the rift in time, but before they were able to do anything I heard shouting from the police and then gunfire, my soldiers falling one by one. I pressed myself back against the brick wall, cursing myself for being so stupid. I should have fashioned them as modern men who fit in with Milltown of today.

I was attempting to conjure more when I saw Airy racing along the sidewalk in front of the college. Two men from the past hurtled after her, knives poised to throw.

I stepped out from my hiding place. "Hey! Over here!" I yelled. A knife zinged by my ear, a second one catching me in the thigh before I could move out of the way. I let out a scream and fell heavily onto the cement, blood pouring from the wound. A moment later Airy was there, her warm hand on my shoulder. "We better get you out of here," she said, clutching her ring.

We whirled through the ether and a moment after that we hit another sidewalk and Airy fell into my arms. "Airy, my gods—where have you been?"

She held me close. "It's a long story," she whispered.

I glanced down the empty street, hearing the wind gathering strength as it whistled around buildings, bringing bits of paper, plastic bags and empty cardboard coffee cups with it. Buildings looked abandoned, trash blowing everywhere, the heavy gray sky adding to the air of desolation. "Where did you take us?"

"Milltown, September of 2200."

"How did you come up with that date? Looks like the rift hasn't been repaired."

"How do you know? Maybe this is another dimension."

I sighed and looked down at the blood oozing from my leg. "Right now I need a doctor who can stitch this up before I bleed to death."

Airy paled, scanning down the abandoned street. "Can you walk? The clinic isn't far. Maybe there are some supplies left."

"Supplies left? From when?"

She frowned at me. "No, not from our time. This place has obviously undergone some changes since then. People have lived here recently. Look around Fehin—do you remember Milltown ever looking like this?"

I scanned the newer buildings made of metal and glass interspersed with a few older ones I remembered. The glass of one had been shattered and littered the sidewalk, bricks of an older building missing and leaving a large hole in the side of what had once been someone's house. The street was wider now, although the asphalt was pulled up and cracked. The park was replaced with an apartment building that towered above us, its windows missing and tattered curtains blowing in the breeze. There were hardly any trees, and what there were, looked nearly dead. "I hope there isn't radiation," I muttered.

She shook her head. "This is not from a nuclear bomb. If it were, there would be nothing here but rubble. This seems more like years of disuse and storms, and maybe a war—hard to tell."

She supported me, the two of us hobbling along the sidewalk. We didn't see another soul, a cat or a dog, or even a rat. When we came to a building with the familiar + sign indicating a clinic, it was not the one I remembered. The door was off its hinges, dry leaves blowing in and out as the breeze came up. The place had been ransacked, any drugs long gone, but still we found a locked case in a back room that held gauze, some antiseptic and a roll of tape. I pulled my sleeve down and smashed the glass before reaching in.

"It needs to be cauterized," I told her once I'd stripped off my jeans and taken a good look. "Otherwise it will continue to bleed."

"How do I do that?"

"With a heat source and something that we can lay along it. Could be a stick if that's all we can find."

"How about this?" she asked, holding up a scalpel.

"Fine, but we need a fire. I can do it with magic if you can help me find some wood."

Airy carried a bottle of alcohol, a roll of tape and one of gauze as she helped me outside again. She left me sitting with my back against a tree and went to find enough wood to make a fire. While she was gone I took off my shirt and tied it tightly above the wound, hoping to stave off the blood loss. I was dozing when she got back and woke to see her placing the wood into a little pyramid.

"I hope it's dry enough to burn," she said, looking up at me worriedly. There had obviously been a rainstorm recently, leaves soaked under trees, puddles filled, roofs still dripping.

Once it was set I waved my hands to get it burning, using more energy than usual because of the wet wood. I let it burn to coals before I instructed her to stick the scalpel in. "Rip a piece of my shirt so you don't burn yourself. That metal will be hot."

She did as I asked and wrapped it around her hand. "What about you? This is going to hurt."

"Hand me that stick," I said, pointing to one that hadn't been put into the fire. "As soon as the metal looks red hot you need to take it out. Press it on my leg in short bursts until it seems like the wound is sealed. Try not to burn the good flesh if you can help it."

"Why don't you instruct me as I do it?"

"Because I may pass out. Whenever you're ready." I placed the stick in my mouth and lay back.

A second later I let out a scream as pain seared through me. I heard Airy crying. "Again, Airy," I muttered, gasping. White-hot pain moved through my leg and this time a blessed darkness rolled over me.

I opened my eyes to see Airy staring down with a frown of worry. "Are you okay?"

I pushed myself up. "I don't know. Did the bleeding stop?" I looked at my leg, which was neatly bandaged. "How long was I out?"

"Ten minutes? I don't know. That was terrible and I never want to do it again."

"Better than bleeding to death," I mumbled, trying to stand.

"Fehin!" She grabbed hold of me as I swayed against her. "You need to wait a minute or two at least." She helped me lower myself to the ground.

"We need supplies, Airy. And we need to figure out how to repair the—"

"Stop," she said, holding up her hand. "Right now you need to rest. I'll scout out a market and see if there's any food to be had, and then we can make a plan. Okay?"

I nodded and tried to smile. She kissed me quickly and hurried away.

"Be careful!" I called, watching her disappear around the corner.

I fell asleep while she was gone, waking to see a couple of shadowy shapes slipping in between buildings across the street. When she arrived a few minutes later I breathed a sigh of relief. "We're not alone," I said, pointing across the street.

"You saw someone?"

"A few someones—they were over there."

She ignored me as she pulled some beef jerky and a bag of corn chips from the plastic bag. "I also found some juice," she said proudly, producing a bottle of cranberry cocktail. "The shelves have been emptied and of course the frozen food is long gone."

It was then that the men I'd seen headed toward us from across the street. "Get us out of here," I hissed. "Now!"

Airy looked up, her eyes going wide. She grabbed my hand.

We were no longer in Milltown, unless a hundred years had gone by and there'd been a nuclear war. This place was stripped of pretty much everything-- no houses, no trees, nothing but dry grasses waving in the cold breeze. Rain was falling from a sullen sky and it was growing dark. "Where are we now?" I asked.

Airy was crying, her hands over her face. "I don't know. I just got us out of there as quickly as I could."

"You don't remember what you said?"

She shook her head.

I grabbed hold of her hand, squeezing her fingers. "It's okay, Airy. Now that you have more control of the ring we can go wherever we want."

"That's just it! The ring got lost on the way. I had it in my hand and then it was gone!"

I stared at her. "Holy shit."

"We're stuck here, Fehin, and we don't know where *here* is!"

"If worse comes to worse the druid will come for us— apparently he always knows exactly what we're up to."

"Worse has already come to worse." She stared at me, her eyes filled with tears. "And it's all my fault."

"Talking about fault doesn't help anything."

Airy scanned into the distance. "Should we search for a village or something? We'll need food and shelter."

"Yeah, sure. While we walk you can tell me about your experience while you were away. But my leg still hurts—not sure how far I can go."

"I'll support you," she said, taking hold of my arm.

As we walked slowly across the grassy hill she began to tell me about the beings of light and what they'd told her.

"They're part of us, a part that a lot of people don't recognize anymore."

"Our divine spark."

"Yeah, I guess that's a good way of putting it, although the word divine conjures a god-like being, not a spark of light."

"That's because the word has been taken over by religions. It was first used to describe soothsayers. It also meant 'to conjure or guess' or have supernatural insight."

"How come you know this stuff?"

"My mom. She was a devout non-Christian." I laughed. "And I studied comparative religions."

"You got a lot more out of six months of college than I did in over a year."

I scanned into the distance. "Does that look like huts to you?"

Airy gazed where I pointed. "It looks like some pre-historic village. What if Neanderthals live there?"

"I think they lived in caves. This has to be later than that. We could be in Mongolia, or maybe it's a native village in Africa or somewhere in the Americas."

"Are we going to walk up and introduce ourselves? There's no place to hide."

"It people are there they've for sure already seen us."A second later an arrow whizzed by my ear. "Yup, they've seen us all right! Come on!" I grabbed her hand and hobbled back in the direction we'd come. But with no trees we were sitting ducks, running or not.

CHAPTER NINE

AIRY

a s we ran I called out to the beings who insisted they were part of me. *Please help us!* I could hear strange sounds behind us, as though our pursuers were chanting in another language, but I didn't look back. The hilly terrain we were on began to descend, and below us I could see a river with trees alongside it. But as we drew closer a blinding light directly above the ground revealed an opening into another world. Clouds roiled over a copse of dark trees, and then suddenly beings were piling toward us through the gap, one after the other. They were enormous and dressed in armor, some with leather, some with chain mail, and they held clubs and bows and arrows, scabbards hanging on their belts.

"Did you do that?" Fehin asked.

"No!" I shouted. "I don't have the ring!"

I felt the pull of Fehin's hand as he dragged me in another direction toward a small group of trees. We stumbled and cut ourselves on briars trying to find cover. I felt like a rabbit being pursued by a fox as we peeked out from our hiding place under some sticker bushes.

The two groups were as different as they could be, one medieval in nature, the other a black-skinned indigenous tribe dressed only in loincloths, streaks of red and white covering their cheeks. I heard shouts from both sides, the twang of bowstrings and the whizz of arrows, followed by screams of pain as they clashed together. The medieval ones had more weaponry and certainly the upper hand, as they slashed with their razor sharp broadswords. "They're killing them!"

Fehin's dark stare met mine. "This is what Gunnar was trying to tell me. This is the rip in time. This is not supposed to happen."

"And I'm supposed to fix it? Is that what you're saying? How, Fehin? I don't even have the damn ring anymore."

"We're the ones who caused it, Airy. I have no solution, but at least now I've seen what he was talking about."

Tears filled my eyes as I watched the native men fall on the field, blood pooling around them. The soldiers who had come through the rift had killed them all and now were heading toward the village. "They're going after the women and children."

Fehin met my gaze, his expression stony. "There is nothing we can do."

"Call Gunnar. We have to get out of here and fix this. Who knows what's happened as a result—the entire world could be completely changed because of my meddling." I was seriously crying now and Fehin put his arm around my shoulders.

"You didn't know," he said softly. "How could you?"

It wasn't long before we heard terrified shrieking in the distance and saw smoke rising from the thatched huts. The worst had happened.

$$\sim$$

It was an hour or more before Gunnar appeared, his eyes narrowed in anger. "So you've finally witnessed your handiwork," he said, staring at Fehin who crouched like a cowering animal. "This is but one skirmish, Fehin. You have no idea what's been happening. The timeline you were in is gone forever."

"It isn't Fehin's fault!" I cried, grabbing his sleeve. "I'm the one who did it, Gunnar."

"What timeline are you talking about?" Fehin asked.

"Future Milltown," the druid answered. "The one you were just in. I have no idea what will happen as a result of this. You should have known better," the druid continued. "You should understand the dangers associated with time travel. I certainly thought I'd impressed it upon you when you were younger."

I took hold of Gunnar's sleeve. "I lost the ring."

Gunnar's frown turned even darker. "You what? Where is it?"

"I dropped it when I was moving through the ether—I have no idea where it is."

The druid stared into space. "This is not good, not good at all. You need the ring to repair what you've done."

"Why can't you repair it?" I asked.

"It isn't that simple, Airy. I am not authorized, nor would I be able to even if I were. You and only you are tasked with this undertaking. The one who caused it is the one who must mend it. And I'm afraid the damage has reached a critical point."

"What about Otherworld and Thule? Are they okay?"

"They are still intact because they lie separate from normal reality. Perhaps I will have to take you there in order to find a way around this problem. You certainly can't be caught up in what's going on in Milltown or any other place on the planet. You saw what happened here—well, it's like that everywhere now."

"Is it only the medieval soldiers? What about the alternate timelines?"

"No. It's much more than that. All timelines are mixed up and some have disappeared altogether. There's war on every continent."

I contemplated the enormity of the problem. "I don't see how I could fix it even if I had the ring."

"The ring is able to mend the tears in time, Airy. Once the rifts you opened are closed the world will come back into balance. "

"But what about all the people who came through from the past? Won't they still be here?"

Gunnar nodded. "You will have to find a way to remove them."

Fehin swiveled to stare at him. "What? That's impossible!"

"It isn't impossible, but it will be difficult. I can search for the ring, but if I don't find it both of you will be called upon to use every bit of magic you've ever had." He glanced at me. "And you, Airy, will need to call on the beings of light you just met. They can help." Gunnar turned to see a group of soldiers heading our way. "But right now I have to take you out of here before we all get killed."

"Where are you taking us?" I asked, but we were already whirling through the ether. I had no desire to go home to Otherworld. The idea of facing my mother right now made me feel sick inside. I could almost see the 'I told you so' look on her face.

⁓

We landed on a beach that I knew with certainty was not in Otherworld. "Is this Thule?"

Fehin nodded. "But it doesn't look right."

I followed his gaze, noticing that it seemed like a hurricane had come through, downed limbs and a mess of detritus along the beach and further inland. Several unusual feathery trees had been uprooted, and lay dead, their leaves shriveled and brown. In the distance toward the mountains it seemed as though gale force winds had flattened every bit of plant life.

Gunnar's face had gone pale. "Something has happened," he said, scanning the area. "Stay here, I have to find out what it is." He disappeared.

"And where does he think we'll go?" I muttered.

"I've got to take a look around," Fehin announced. "Do you want to stay and wait or come with?"

"I'm coming with you." He hobbled away and I followed, hoping we wouldn't suddenly discover the ravaged skeletons of his mother and Kafir. I was tired of blood and death, the feeling that all of it was my fault.

"It's like there was never a village here," Fehin said, heading under the tall trees that remained. "My animals are all gone, including the dragons." After walking for a while we came upon a different type of tree, one with wide limbs like an oak. "This is where Kafir built the tree house where he and my mom live. There's no sign of any of it."

"So what does it mean?"

Fehin shrugged. "It must have something to do with the time anomalies. I guess we'll have to wait for Gunnar to come back."

I glanced at his worried expression. "At least they aren't all dead," I said, trying to be upbeat.

He stared at me, his eyes bleak. "We *hope* they aren't."

A few minutes later Gunnar appeared. "All are safe in the past. I took us too far ahead in time."

Fehin visibly relaxed. "But how can the future be like this?" he asked, gesturing. "It's like the village was never here."

Gunnar let out a sigh. "I don't know, Fehin. I have a feeling it's related to—"

"To what I did," I said in a small voice. And then I was sobbing. "What have I done?" Gunnar touched me on the arm and held out his hand. In his palm was my ring. "You found it!"

He nodded. "Pure luck, believe me."

"The beings of light were helping you," I said, sliding it on my finger. "I'm never taking it off again." I looked at Gunnar. "Now, tell us how to mend the gaps in time."

It took more than an hour before Gunnar was finished giving us our assignment. We sat on the beach staring out to sea as he talked, happy to hear the screech of seabirds and see the foam of white caps appear and disappear as the breeze freshened. A moment of calm in a world gone mad. When he was finished my head felt woozy with it all, and when I glanced at Fehin the expression on his face told me he felt the same. "So first we have to go back to the beginning—the first place we went? How in the world can I find it?"

"You have to concentrate on one thing specific for each timeline. For instance, you told me about the man and woman appearing—concentrate on them, or you can concentrate on Merlin."

"Where did we go after that?" I asked Fehin.

"We went to the place with the fake trees, didn't we?"

"Oh yeah. Mr. Sand." I felt sick remembering.

"You can think of Mr. Sand. That will at least get you there. And before you leave each place you have to use your ring to close the gap in time." He took hold of my hand and moved it to show me. "You move it in a counter-clockwise circle just before you step through the rift. And you must ask the beings of light to assist you in making sure every one is closed. I know it sounds difficult, but you'll get the hang of it."

"Difficult? It sounds impossible! Why can't you help us?"

Gunnar looked aggrieved for a moment. "I would if I could, Airy. I'm afraid this is not my purview and goes against certain laws that cannot be broken."

I glanced at Fehin. "So I guess we need to start in Milltown? That's where we left from the first time."

"Correct. And make very sure that you close them in sequence. If you do one before another it could create even more anomalies." He stared into the distance before turning back to us. "I have to warn you that this will be dangerous. Every timeline has been altered now, and you don't know what you might find. It could be confusing. When you leave for the past you don't need to close the gaps with the ring--

only use it when you travel from past to future. Do you understand?"

The expression on his face told me this was of the utmost importance. I didn't want to know what would happen if I made a mistake and did it backwards. I nodded.

"Okay. Let's go. I'll drop you off in Milltown and you can take it from there."

Fehin took hold of my hand, his fingers twining through mine. When I glanced at him his eyes were dark with worry. A moment later we whirled into the ether.

CHAPTER TEN
FEHIN

Gunnar dropped us off in Milltown and disappeared, leaving us in the midst of a riot. Police threw tear gas, sirens blared, people fought with sticks and clubs and the sound of shooting could be heard further up the street. When I reached for Airy's hand she was gone, sucked into the mob. And when I went to find her I couldn't see her anywhere. I tried to stay separate from the chaos, knowing that if I caught up in that mass of humanity I could very well be trampled or beaten to a pulp by the crazed men and women who were fighting.

I moved backward, hugging the buildings, and followed slowly, trying to locate her as I attempted to make sense of what was happening. It seemed that three different groups were fighting: Milltown residents, the people who wore the indigo tunics, and some other group that almost seemed prehistoric from their enormous size and lack of clothing.

They had massive heads and wore wild animal skins, their shoulders a good ten inches wider than normal shoulders. And they were armed with clubs. The screaming made me want to plug my ears. People were on the ground, many not moving, others trying to crawl away, and in the distance I could see the police in riot gear marching in a line, their stun guns stopping people in their tracks.

When I caught a glimpse of red hair I ran forward, trying to stay close to the buildings so as not to get pulled into the fray, but seeing Airy being carried along changed my mind. A moment later I was in the thick of it, working my way toward her and being pummeled, kicked and hit with sticks as I struggled through it all. "Airy!" I screamed.

She turned, her face as white as I'd ever seen it, and then I watched her fall. *Airy I'm coming—hang on.* But by the time I got to where she'd been there was no sign of her, either on the ground or in the crowd. I heard an explosion and watched smoke pour out of one of the buildings, glass shattering and hurtling toward the crowd. I ducked and held my hands over my face, only to be hit by one of the giants and thrown to the ground. He stepped on my hurt leg and kept going, his face a mask of fury. I let out a scream of pain that was lost in the chaos, trying to rise. But every time I reached my knees another group came by, knocking me flat. I curled up in a ball waiting for an opportunity and hoping there would be one before I was trampled to death.

I heard gunshots, uncovering my eyes to see several giants falling like tree trunks, blood pouring from their chests. A roar went through the crowd, everyone seeming to galvanize against the police. The movement was like a tidal wave and when it reached the line of cops their guns became useless. I watched them mowed down like so many stick figures as the crowd surged forward. I stood and hurried after the crowd, trying to spot Airy. When I saw her she was being held like a rag doll, bright hair cascading over the enormous arm. She was in the arms of a giant and it looked like she was either injured or possibly dead. She certainly wasn't conscious. I worked my way out of the thinning crowd and moved toward her as quickly as I could, considering the condition of my leg. The wound had been opened again, blood trickling down and into my boot. And it hurt like holy hell.

The giant turned as I approached, his eyes glazed and uncomprehending. I pointed to Airy. "She's mine," I said, holding out my arms.

He grunted and stared and I knew he had no idea what I said. I pointed to Airy and placed a hand on my chest. "Mine," I said again. Something seemed to register in his brain as he turned to see several of his compatriots lying on the ground. He frowned. And then he put Airy gently down on the ground in front of me. A moment later he was on his knees trying to rouse another giant who was obviously dead. Tears sprang into my eyes as he picked the woman up and carried her away.

I pressed fingers to Airy's neck, checking for a pulse. It was thready but at least she was alive. Some of the chaos had diminished in the last few minutes, probably because so many people were lying dead, including many members of the police force. And then I saw it—the brightness blinding me before the rift opened in the distance, enormous rhinos and tigers and other prehistoric beasts rushing through. I picked Airy up and ran as fast as I could manage toward the college and the woods behind.

"Airy, wake up!" I slapped her face and shook her. Then I examined her for wounds, bruising, or other reasons why she might still be unconscious, and found a large bump on the back of her head. I sat against a tree and cradled her in my lap wondering what to do. If she had bleeding in her brain it was seriously dangerous, but venturing toward a hospital or clinic was out of the question right now. I heard animals snuffling in the woods, knowing that I was definitely one of their food sources. I picked up Airy and headed toward the entrance to the college. There was a clinic there.

"How did you get in here?" the woman at the front desk asked. "I was sure I locked that door."

I didn't want to tell her I'd used magic to open it, so feigning innocence I said, "It was open when I came through."

She jumped up and hurried to the door and locked it from the inside. "I don't know how that happened," I heard her mutter. "Now what do you want? And what's wrong with this girl you brought in? Do you think I can help her? Because if you do you're sadly mistaken." She glanced toward the door, as the noise seemed to penetrate into the hallway. "They can't get in here," she murmured, her eyes wide.

"You're safe," I assured her. "At least for the time being. Where is the clinic?"

Her gaze returned to me. "You can't access it from in here, and even if you could there's no one on duty."

"Crap."

Her gaze went to Airy in my arms. "Not sure what to say—there's been a lot of death out there. I'm terrified to leave this place and if I don't get out of here soon I'll starve to death. I would suggest getting out of town as quickly as you can."

"That won't do any good; the unrest is everywhere."

"Why? What's happening?"

I shook my head. "Too complicated to explain. I'll let myself out."

By the time I was outside again Airy was beginning to wake up. I saw a tiger run by on the street and heard the roar as it leapt into the air, hysterical shrieking a moment later. The animals were definitely adding to the pandemonium. I went behind the college administration building and put Airy on the ground. "Are you okay?" I asked as her eyes fluttered open.

Her hand went to the back of her head. "Someone hit me hard enough to knock me out. Where are we? What's going on?"

"You mean besides the Neanderthals, the sabre toothed tigers and the woolly rhinos roaming the streets of Milltown?"

She stared at me. "We didn't go to a timeline that had those. How did they get here?"

"I don't know and I don't care, other than us doing what we came here for. Getting the animals out of here is not a task I look forward to."

Airy rubbed the back of her head, her gaze going to my leg. "You're bleeding."

"Actually I think it's stopped now. The blood on my jeans is from earlier. Can we concentrate on closing the rips in time?"

She scoffed. "We can try, but I think Gunnar is crazy if he thinks we can stop what's going on. Did you believe him when he said he wasn't authorized to help? Really?"

"I know nothing about it, Airy. But I suggest we get on it before we have more bedlam here. Three quarters of the police force is dead and I can't even count how many others. The animals are all over town attacking and killing other animals as well as people. The entire place has gone nuts."

Airy stood, swaying into me. "I feel dizzy."

I held onto her. "All we have to do is travel backward in time to where we were and then come forward and mend the rips we made."

"Yeah. It's nothing the dynamic duo can't handle," she said sarcastically.

"Come on," I said, tugging her by the arm. "The sooner we go the sooner things will get back to normal."

She rubbed her ring, thinking. "First we were with Merlin, right?"

I nodded.

"Okay." She took hold of my hand. "I'm picturing him in my mind and I'm picturing those cool woods with the squirrel and the man and woman who were…"

A second later we whirled through darkness and a second after that we thumped into the town square, exactly where we'd been when Merlin got us out of there. Except this time there was no market going on. I heard the clash of swords in the distance. Shouting. "War here too?"

"Not exactly war," I heard a male voice say. "I thought I got the two of ye out of here."

"We had to come back and fix what we messed up," Airy said. "Who's fighting?"

"Some dark-skinned tribes I've never seen before and the knights from the castle. It isn't going well for the tribes."

I turned to Airy. "They came through the time rift."

Merlin watched us. "And you're here to fix it."

"How am I supposed to do this, Fehin? Do we have to go back to the present every time, or do I repair it as we go on to the next place?"

"We have to go back to the present, Airy. Gunnar said if we do it the other way it could cause more problems."

"So it has to be past to present, not present to past."

"Correct."

"To Milltown again? I don't want to go there."

"Sorry," I said, watching her debate the issue in her mind.

"Good luck to the both of ye," Merlin said. "And if ye come upon that time-travelin' druid, give him my regards." A half second later he wasn't there.

"Why couldn't he help us? He has magic," Airy asked, annoyed.

"Because we did it and we need to repair it. Now stop complaining and let's get to it."

"I hope this works," she said. She took the stone off her finger and began the circling Gunnar had told her to do, her brows furrowed. It was several moments of this before the rift opened. We hurtled through.

CHAPTER ELEVEN

AIRY

I looked around. "This isn't Milltown. Where are we now?" I muttered. A steep cliff rose up behind us, ledges of rock stair-stepping up toward jagged peaks that rose like broken teeth into a sky dark with cloud. In front of us flat grassland stretched into the distance where herds of animals grazed. "Are those buffalo?"

Fehin sat up and rubbed his shoulder where a tear in his shirt showed a bright red spot. "What were you thinking when you brought us here? It sure wasn't anything about Milltown."

"I was fighting with myself about Milltown—I didn't want to go back but I knew we had to—maybe some other thoughts crept in."

Fehin frowned, staring at me. "Like what, Airy?"

"So now you're mad at me? I'm sorry I don't have perfect control of my every thought like you do."

Fehin sighed heavily and pressed his lips together. "I didn't say that. But every time something like this happens it screws it all up—don't you see? If this is further in the past than the last timeline, we just did exactly what Gunnar warned against."

I closed my eyes realizing he was right. "How can we tell?"

"I guess we need to identify what's grazing out there—that might give us a clue."

"I remember I was thinking how nice it would be to go to a place where there were no people."

"No people--that's the thought you had when we were supposed to go to Milltown? Are we back before people existed, or what?"

I shrugged. "Let's take a look at the animals," I answered, brushing off my jeans before heading toward them. I felt like a complete idiot and if Fehin said one more word I would surely burst into tears.

It took an hour before we got close enough to identify the herds. There were a couple of deer species and some others that looked like a cross between a wildebeest and a giraffe. Others were pig-like with tusks. "Not sure identifying them is going to help," I said, turning to Fehin.

"I've never seen anything like those," Fehin said, pointing to the wildebeest/giraffe. "The piggy ones look like your average wild boar, but those..." he shook his head.

"Could we be in a fake place—I mean one that I conjured?"

Fehin's eyebrows went up. "Have you ever conjured anything?"

"Well, no, but— " I heard a sound and looked back at the mountains, noticing half a dozen men climbing along the cliffs.

"So much for no people," Fehin said, staring at me. "They have spears—get us out of here."

"So, do I--?"

"Airy, just take us back to Milltown. Now!"

This time there was no rift, nothing but the ether, and a moment later we were on the streets of Milltown faced with the same pandemonium as before. At least we weren't right in the middle of it, but when the rift opened and the men we'd just seen poured out Fehin grabbed my arm.

"Take us to Mr. Sand's world!" he shouted. "We can mend the rift when we come back again!"

One of the natives had his spear up ready to throw when we whirled into the darkness.

"That was too close," Fehin muttered after we landed. And then I heard him gasp. "Airy! Look where we are!"

We were standing in the parlor, Mr. Sand glaring at us from his place by the fire. "That's a neat trick," he said, his eyes glittering. "Something else I can use for a selling point. Now come along, children. I have buyers waiting."

Before I could do anything he'd separated us as neatly as slicing a loaf of bread. He laughed, watching my face. "Give me that ring."

Instead of complying I moved one half hour into the future. But when I arrived back in the same spot, Fehin was gone and so was Mr. Sand. When I searched through the house I couldn't find either one of them.

"What are *you* doing here?" I heard the maid ask.

I turned. "Where is Fehin?"

She laughed. "He's been taken to auction. And if you stay around you'll be on the block as well."

"Where is it and how do I get there?"

"You won't find it before you're picked up and taken to jail. You have to have a number to be on the street." She showed me the inside of her arm where several numbers had been tattooed in blue ink.

I tried to think but my mind refused to work. Maybe if I went back to Milltown, closed the rift, and then returned earlier I'd be in time to save him. I rubbed my ring and thought about Milltown, and when the rift opened I moved the ring counter clockwise, forgetting completely that I had to come back to this time line to save Fehin. And just before I spun away the maid grabbed hold of my arm and spun out with me.

When we landed in Milltown the woman stared around in terror. "Where have you brought me?" A rhino ran by chased by a tiger and behind them came a man with a spear, his high-pitched hunting cry splitting the air. In the distance the fighting still raged, and if anything it seemed worse than before. And it looked like a storm was about to hit, the sky dark with cloud, cold wind whipping the hair back from my face.

"You shouldn't have grabbed me," I told her, trying to decide what to do. "I have to go back because I did it wrong."

"Did what wrong? Are you a sorceress?"

"You have magic in that horrible world you live in?"

She shrugged. "If they're caught they're turned loose and hunted for sport." She gazed up the street, watching the mayhem. "I will not go back," she announced.

"You'd rather stay here?" I asked, shocked.

"At least I'm free. There is no fighting where I live because there is nothing to gain by it."

"Suit yourself," I said, trying to decide how to picture where I wanted to be. I thought of the room with the fireplace and pictured Fehin and Mr. Sand standing there, and rubbed the stone with my forefinger.

It was less than thirty seconds later that a hand clamped down on my arm so hard I let out a cry. Mr. Sand stared into my face, his piggy eyes narrowed. "Give me that ring—now!"

"Fehin—grab my hand!" But before he could do so, Mr. Sand had pulled it off my finger.

He stared at it, his eyes gleaming. "Tell me how it works."

"It only works for me."

"I don't believe you—tell me!" he shouted, twisting my arm in a grip of iron.

"Give it to me and I'll show you," I said, glancing at Fehin.

Mr. Sand stared at me. "I'm not stupid enough to fall for that one."

"I can take you with me if you like," I said. "All you have to do is touch my arm."

He moved closer, his hand still gripping my upper arm. "Show me," he said as he handed me the stone.

I slipped it on, visualizing the plains, the mountains, and the men with spears. When we landed it was just as it was when Fehin and I left, the men crawling down the rock face, spears at the ready. Mr. Sand looked around in horror and moved backward, letting go of my arm as he watched the men advancing. "Where have you taken me?"

"To a place where you're the prey," I said, rubbing my ring as I pictured Fehin and the drawing room, the fireplace. Less than a second later I whirled away.

"My gods, Airy! Quick thinking!" Fehin said when I landed in the room. "Where did you leave him?"

I smiled. "With the animals and the natives with spears. He'll be hunted just as the people here are hunted. What a fitting end to an evil man."

He grabbed me and pulled me to him. "I'm sorry for doubting you—that was some fast maneuvering."

"I think I'm getting the hang of it. Let's get out of here." I waited for the rift to open and spent several minutes turning the stone in a counter clockwise circle before we moved into the ether. And this time I had the feeling I'd closed the gap to Mr. Sand's world—hopefully for good.

Milltown was still a mess, and now there were tanks running around shooting at the animals that had obviously killed and disemboweled several people. Hysteria had reached a fever pitch and it seemed that the mayhem had spread everywhere, smoke rising in the distance as houses were torched, people running for their lives. Fehin took my hand as we circumnavigated the bodies, trying not to look down. The stench was horrific.

"How in hell are we going to get these animals out of here?" Fehin hissed, stepping around a particularly gruesome body.

I shook my head, about to retch. "For now I'd rather concentrate on closing the tears. Maybe the tank guys will slaughter all of them."

"Where to now?"

"Do you think we have to go back to the African plains where the spear men were?"

"If they're here in the present then we have to go back and close it."

I nodded, not wanting to think about Mr. Sand. "So that's the last one." It was then that I recognized the maid who had come through the rift with me. She lay on her back in a pool of blood, her eyes wide and staring. "Oh no."

Fehin came close. "Isn't that--?"

"Yes. She thought she could have a better life."

"That sucks," Fehin said, stepping around her. He shook his head and looked away. "I'm ready when you are," he said.

I was so upset it was hard for me to concentrate, and as we left the present I was afraid my thoughts had turned to matters they shouldn't have. And when we landed it became instantly obvious.

Fehin looked at me. "Okay, this isn't..."

"I know," I said, noticing the smoke rising in the distance. "We didn't close this one," I said, trying to cover for my unruly thoughts. "Before we leave I want to see if there's anything we can do to help."

"Airy, I don't think that's a good—"

I stared at him defiantly. "I don't care. What happened to them is my fault." I headed toward the dark cloud on the horizon, hoping that at least a few people in the village were still alive. I now knew how to cauterize wounds, a skill I was sure would come in handy.

I was staring at my feet when I heard Fehin shout, "Watch out!" I looked up to see the soldiers wearing armor moving toward me, bows and arrows poised to shoot. I ran toward Fehin and grabbed his hand. "If I work it right I can send them back into their timeline," I gasped.

"Trouble is if you let them get that close we could get shot."

I asked the beings of light for help, muttering to myself as we ran. Near the mountain range I stopped and rubbed the stone. Immediately the rift opened up, revealing a verdant green valley with low hills, a castle on the far ridge. "This is where they came from," I said, glancing at Fehin.

Fehin looked over his shoulder just as an arrow hissed by his ear. "I say get a move on and hope the gap doesn't close before they get here!" he shouted, pulling me forward toward the gaping hole.

We plunged through, and a minute later the soldiers came after us. I couldn't see how many since I was running for my life.

"Once they're all in we need to close it, Airy!" Fehin yelled, glancing at me as he ran. His face was red, his breath coming in gasps.

I glanced over my shoulder counting. Around twenty I figured—not all of them, but enough. As soon as the rift closed I rubbed the stone and visualized Milltown replete with beasts--how it had been the last time we were there. As soon as it opened again I circled the stone in a counter-clockwise motion before moving through. Fehin came after me and the hole closed just after an arrow hit Fehin in the arm.

We landed in a heap in the copse of trees behind the college. Fehin was grunting in pain, the arrow deeply imbedded in the muscle of his upper arm. Blood trickled down, turning his shirt a deep red.

"How do I get it out?"

"You have to pull it out, Airy," he groaned.

"I can't!" I said, staring down at the wooden shaft, the metal buried in his flesh.

"The good thing is this is a straightforward arrow with no barbs."

"How do you know?"

"Because that's what they used back then. If it was barbed I'd know it, believe me." He looked up, his eyes dulled with pain.

I tried not to think as I grabbed hold of the shaft and pulled straight up as hard as I could. I heard Fehin suck in breath and the sob that escaped his lips as the arrow released, sending me sprawling. By the time I had risen to my knees Fehin was ashen, his eyes closed. The wound was pouring blood in rhythm to his heartbeat. It must have hit a vessel. I pulled off my shirt and ripped a strip of cloth and tied it as tightly as I could above the wound.

"Airy," Fehin said, weakly. "You're going to have to do the cauterizing again. If you don't I'll bleed to death."

I slowly shook my head, trying to think of another way.

"Please, Airy. Get some wood and use the arrow head," he gasped. "And hurry."

There was no other way, I realized, as I searched frantically for limbs and sticks dry enough to burn. Once I had enough I did what I'd done the last time, forming them into a small pyramid. "Can you use your magic to start the fire?" I asked, shaking him by the shoulder.

He tried several times before the wood caught and began to smolder. Meanwhile his face was so white I wondered if he had any blood left in his body. He was unconscious by the time the fire was hot enough to heat up the arrowhead--a blessing, really.

I placed the tip into the flames until it was white-hot, and then I held it against the bleeding wound, hoping it would work. The last time there hadn't been this much blood. The caustic stench of burning flesh made me feel sick as I moved the arrowhead back into the fire and repeated the process. I did this at least four times before I sat back on my heels to see if it worked. The blood had congealed now, Fehin's shirt and jeans soaked with it. He had not regained consciousness.

As I waited for him to wake up the sounds of the ongoing chaos reached my ears. I had been so concentrated on what I was doing I hadn't heard it at all. Now it arrived full-blown, as though a radio had been turned on full blast. Despite our efforts, nothing in Milltown had changed. And now Fehin was injured and we had to get these animals out of here. I cradled his head in my lap and called to the light beings. *Please help us.*

But instead of the light beings Gunnar appeared, his eyes dark with rage. "You have not done what you need to do, Airy."

"I've been trying, but it's hard. I have no idea how to get the animals out of here."

"Do you realize you've opened several other rifts? If you don't close them soon there will be no turning back."

"Did you happen to notice Fehin lying here?" I shouted. "He got hit by an arrow."

Gunnar looked down. "If you'd timed things better it wouldn't have happened."

"Damn you, Gunnar!" I yelled, but he had already disappeared.

"What did *he* want?" Fehin muttered.

"To make me feel bad? Honestly, I have no idea." I bent to place a kiss on his forehead. "I'm glad you're awake, Fehin. You lost a lot of blood."

"I know—I can feel it. If you want to leave me here and do your thing I'm okay with that."

"I'm not leaving you anywhere. Gunnar seems to think we've done even more damage, but of course, he didn't explain how to fix it."

"I don't remember opening up any more rifts, other than the ones we've been closing," Fehin mumbled. "I need to sleep for a while. Maybe you can scout around for something to eat—I need to build up my blood."

I wondered how I could reach the market in the chaos. But I did as he asked, leaving him to rest as I worked my way carefully toward the street.

It was growing dark by the time I got back with a stale loaf of bread, a packet of peanut butter crackers and one of cheese. But it wasn't dark enough to hide the tiger lying next to Fehin. I stopped dead in my tracks, staring at the enormous beast with the razor sharp tusks protruding from its mouth.

Fehin was sitting up, his hand on the beast's back. "Don't worry—he's under my control. You do remember I'm a dragon master, right? I have a way with animals."

"I guess you do," I said, moving cautiously forward. "But I don't."

"Yes, you do, Airy. Anyone who can talk to trees can talk to animals as well. Try it out—say something to him in your mind."

The only thing I could think to say was *hi kitty* as I stared stupidly into the golden/amber eyes. The cat blinked once and turned to Fehin.

"He heard you," Fehin said. "Now give me the food— I'm dying here."

"Won't the cat—"

"He's eaten already," Fehin said, ripping open the cheese crackers.

I thought of the half-eaten bodies strewn across the road that I'd avoided on my way to and from the market. "Why is he here?"

"He came to have me for dinner but I stopped him. These creatures are as confused and frightened as the people. Now that we have him he can help us get the rest of them out of here."

"I hope we do it before he gets hungry again."

CHAPTER TWELVE

FEHIN

The cat settled as soon as I spoke to him, my hand in the air to keep him from coming any closer. His fur was matted with blood, rough and torn from many fights, one ear hanging lower than the other. He was upset, all his instincts screaming at once. This was not his home. "Stay here and I'll send you back where you belong," I told him. When Airy arrived he was lying next to me and I could tell from her expression on her face she was terrified of him—and for good reason. His teeth could rip the heart out of just about anything. But with the tanks still roaming the streets, many of his kind had already been killed. It was time to get the rest of them back where they belonged.

I dug into the crackers with gusto, my body demanding sustenance. I couldn't remember the last time I'd had anything to eat.

"Can he contact the others of his kind so that when we open the rift they'll follow him in?"

"Cats are normally solitary, but in this case I think it will work. Just give me tonight to rest and we can get on with it first thing in the morning."

"You're planning to sleep with that thing here?" Airy asked, sitting on the other side of me.

"He won't hurt us, Airy. I've made sure of that."

"And his buddies? What if they come upon us and don't feel so benevolent?"

"They won't because this guy won't let them. We belong to him now."

"Oh great—we're his next kill, is that it?"

I laughed. "Trust me, Airy. He won't hurt us and neither will any of the others. You can sleep knowing that you're safe."

She didn't look convinced as she settled close to me, her wary gaze on the tiger. I handed her a peanut butter cracker.

I slept soundly, waking to see the cat still lying next to me. Airy was gone. I managed to get to my feet and head under the trees to take a wiz, but when I got back Airy still wasn't there. *Airy? Where are you?*

I'm here.

I looked up to see her in the crook of the tree. "Did you sleep up there?"

"Sort of."

"Don't you realize that cats can climb?"

She grinned sheepishly. "Yeah, but it just felt safer. I couldn't close my eyes down there."

"Come on down—we have work to do."

I tried to tell the cat what we were about to do, enlisting his help to get the other cats on board. I hoped he got the gist of it. The rhinos were another matter. He padded ahead of us, his roars grabbing the attention of several people who fled quickly. But the sound drew others of his kind, and by the time Airy had the rift open there were many running toward us. "Lead the way," I told the tiger, grabbing Airy's hand to pull her out of the way. He gave me one last look before leaping through, the others following him. A second later several rhinos appeared, eyeing us before following the tigers into the rift. A few Neanderthals ran by after that, jumping in after them, their eyes wild.

Once the rift closed Airy breathed a sigh of relief. "That was way easier than I expected," Airy said, pushing the hair back from her pale sweaty face. "Glad some of the giants got out of here alive. I thought they'd all been mowed down by the police."

"It's only because we opened the rift here instead of where all the fighting is still going on, not to mention the tiger calling to the others. The rhinos and Neanderthals were an added bonus." I grinned at her.

"You're feeling better," Airy said, staring at me in surprise.

"I feel righteous about saving those prehistoric creatures. And I got a good night's rest, and thanks to you, some food."

"A good night's rest lying next to a creature that could have had you for a midnight snack." She came close to examine my arm. "Amazing what a good burning will do."

I held my arm out to see the wound. "Glad it worked. What do you think Gunnar was talking about? Do we need to revisit what we've already done?"

"I hate to say it, but I think we should check around town and see who's still here."

Fifteen minutes later we were skulking around corners attempting to get a glimpse of what was happening. The tanks plowed up and down the main road, guns sweeping. Shouting could be heard in different places in the city. But when a group of half-dressed street urchins ran by carrying knives I turned. "Who are they?"

Airy had a peculiar look on her face as she watched them. "I think I know what Gunnar was referring to. Remember that timeline we only stayed in for like a minute? I think those kids came from there."

"What's so bad about them?"

"Besides the fact that they're cannibals?"

"What do we do?"

"We have to get them back into that timeline and seal up the rift. But I have no frame of reference for how to get there."

"Try to remember one significant thing about it and concentrate on that."

Airy shook her head. "I don't remember much, other than the thatch on the huts."

"How did you know they were cannibals?"

"Because I saw one of them eating another--didn't you see it?"

"I saw one of them knife the other but I didn't see that. Maybe you should concentrate on that, then."

"Yuck, Fehin!"

I watched the kids advancing on some unsuspecting person who had their back turned. One of them threw a knife and a scream rent the air as the man went down. A second later the kids swarmed over him.

"Oh my gods," Airy said, her eyes flooding.

"Leave it for now," I said, pulling her toward a woman dressed in indigo. "We have to get the indigos back where they belong."

When Airy saw where I was headed she balked and pulled away. "No. I can't go back there again. There's only one of her here—can't we just leave it the way it is? I closed that gap really well."

"You want to talk to her and see if she'd prefer to stay here? Or we can take her somewhere else in the future. Mr. Sand's world is pretty harsh."

Airy let out a reluctant sigh and nodded. When we reached the woman she seemed dazed, staring into space with a blank look on her face. She jumped when Airy touched her arm. "I can take you back to your own time," Airy told her. "But if you'd prefer to stay here that's possible too."

The woman's dark hair had pulled free from her braid and hung in damp wisps around a face covered in scratches. She cradled her right arm against her body. Her tunic was torn in several places, her skirt in tatters around bare feet that were cut and bleeding. "I have lost my man," she said, looking blankly around. "Have you seen him?"

Airy shook her head. "Do you want to go home?"

"Yes," she said.

I drew close and put a hand on Airy's arm. "We can take her into Mr. Sand's world, but a year or so later."

"What good would that do—and how am I supposed to do it?"

"The same way you moved a half hour ahead."

Airy shook her head, her gaze on the ground. "I had a point of reference that time. This time I don't." She looked at me, her eyes bleak. "I hoped I'd never have to see that place again."

"Why? What is so wrong?" the woman asked, brown eyes filling with tears.

"Your people hunt humans for sport. The ones in power are cruel. It's a horrible place to live!"

"It is home," she responded angrily. "And they only hunt the ones who have no means. What else is there to do with them? They are a drag on the society. And now that I no longer have my man I want to be in a familiar place. This world is crazy with its police and guns and those giant machines that kill. So many of us have died here. How can you think this world is any better? All I see is death and destruction."

Airy sighed, glancing at me before turning to the woman. "Take hold of my shoulder and don't let go."

I grabbed her other hand as she began fiddling with her ring. The blinding light came a moment later and Airy pulled us with her into the swirling mass. But as we moved through, my grip loosened, and a moment later I was spinning alone in a dark void, panic filling my body as I tried to make sense of what was happening.

CHAPTER THIRTEEN
AIRY

Somehow in the midst of that momentary leap through time Fehin's fingers slipped from mine. When I found myself in the parlor again Mr. Sand was still there. I must have arrived *before* I moved him into the other timeline. And in my haste I'd visualized him here. Damn! The woman who had come through with me let out a gasp. "I'm not with her," she said, looking around wildly.

"Go," he told her, waving his hand. I watched her run toward the front door and fling it open. A second later the door slammed and she was gone.

I was rubbing my ring and saying the words when he grabbed my hand and tugged the ring off. "Not so fast," he said, shoving my ring into his pocket. "You've already pulled one disappearing act on me and I don't fancy another. Not sure how you do it, but I would wager that moonstone ring has something to do with it." He patted his pocket, smiling smugly. "Now where is your friend? The brothel would pay a lot for a pair. You could perform together and really increase sales. It could be fun for you." He laughed nastily. "I have plans for you, unless you'd rather stay here with me. Which would you prefer, Airy?"

I couldn't answer, sickened by my utter idiocy. Fehin was right. I couldn't control the time travel at all. Tears sprang into my eyes. I wished I knew where Fehin was. This had never happened before and I was at a loss as to how to solve it. Without my ring there was no point in even thinking about it, unless Gunnar came to the rescue. And I doubted that he would, considering how angry he'd been the last time I'd seen him.

I was about to make a run for the front door when he grabbed me around the waist and pulled a hood over my head. I struggled and stumbled trying to get it off, but by that time he'd tied a rope around my hands. And a moment later I was hauled out the door, very nearly falling on my face as he pulled me down the steps. "Step up," he hissed, pushing me into a waiting vehicle. I heard him get in and close the door. *Fehin?* I called in my mind. But he didn't answer. I listened to Mr. Sand's wheezing breath on the seat next to me, the clip-clop of the horse taking me toward a fate I didn't want to think about.

"Where are we going?" I finally managed to ask.

"You'll find out soon enough."

We went on like that for a while before the cart came to an abrupt halt. "Here we are, my dear. Now let's see what I can get for you."

He dragged me from the carriage. "Steps," he called out just as I stumbled against something hard. "Lift your feet."

As soon as we were inside he took the hood off, giving me my first view of the auction hall. Others in my same predicament cast around with stares of fear, their hands tied just as mine were as they were dragged along. At the far end of the room was a stage and on it was the auctioneer, his voice echoing as he described the naked woman standing there. I cringed back from the scene,

terrified, but Mr. Sand pushed me forward. "Won't be long now," he hissed, chuckling in my ear.

Skylights flooded the room with hazy dust motes, illuminating the dark floors that seemed to be made of linoleum. Chairs faced the stage, at least one hundred of them, filled with men and women holding paddles, raising them as they made their bids. They wore all manner of dress, from the bright outfits I'd seen early on, to the indigo blue tunics, to plain brown hooded capes. It wasn't long before a price had been settled on, the woman taken off the stage and given over to an obese older man. I hoped she would be used for domestic work and not forced into a brothel.

Mr. Sand tugged me forward onto the stage. He untied my hands. "Strip," he ordered before backing away. When I didn't comply a man standing in the shadows came forward and did it for me, his hands rough and unfeeling as he pulled off my jeans and tugged my shirt over my head. The underwear was next, and when I fought him he grabbed my arms, pinning them behind me as another man stripped me naked. My protests were silenced by a hard slap to my face.

I had never felt so exposed in all my life, and it wasn't just my lack of clothing. There was something about the entire procedure, the way the audience viewed me as though I was a piece of meat, an animal to be used in whatever manner they wished. I tried to still my fast beating heart as I watched the crowd, hoping for a friendly face. There were none. I would be out of here by now if I had my ring. Would I ever get it back? Panic moved up my throat like a hissing serpent, and for a moment I thought I would throw-up. I tried to run off the stage, but before I reached the edge of the stage the man in the shadows dragged me back. And this time he stayed put behind me. "You'll do well to behave," he muttered in my ear. "This is not the worst of it, believe me."

"...could be used in the household as a maid or in a brothel to serve your special customers..." I heard the auctioneer say. "A playmate for the head of the house, perhaps? ...lovely red hair on this one--very unusual. How much will you give for her? I start the bidding at 1000 huntsman. Can anyone give me 1500?"

I dimly heard the bidding, my attention on the goose bumps rising on my skin, the sensation of many eyes moving across my body. I thought of Fehin, wondering how I would ever find him. Without the ring I was stuck here. And then the bidding was over and I was being led down the steps to the waiting couple who purchased me. They were middle-aged, both with graying hair, and I didn't like the avid look in their eyes. "You will do well by us," the woman said, looking me over, "or you will be turned out to be hunted. Do you understand?"

"What will my job be?"

She scoffed. "We own a brothel and you will be the main draw. No one here has hair your color."

They pulled a cape around my shoulders, re-tied my hands, and led me down a long hall and out the door into the street. Women in indigo rushed along the sidewalk, gazes averted, as though if they made eye contact they would be next on the auction block. Mr. Sand appeared behind us, his expression smug as he looked up and down the street as though he owned it. For one second our eyes met. He smiled, his eyebrows rising in delight. He held up the bag of money he'd gotten for me before turning away, walking with his head held high. I noticed others like him who strutted and seemed above everyone else. Were they the cops of this place, politicians, or what? But my thoughts were cut short when I was roughly hauled into a carriage. A minute later we were clattering down the street to a destination I didn't want to contemplate. I leaned out the window to retch, heartsick and terrified as we hurtled by blank-faced houses, people huddled in doorways and screaming that defied the imagination.

"Get back in here," the woman said, jerking on my arm.

I fell against the seat, trying to control the sickness that was overwhelming me. "I get carsick," I muttered.

"We'll be there in a minute," she said coldly. "If you can't control yourself there are worse things than working in the brothels. Don't test me."

What worse things could there be? I supposed running for your life from hunters could be worse, but that was not what she was talking about. No. The way she said it conjured a dark dungeon and the smell of excrement. I was having a vision and I didn't want to see what lay in the shadows beyond the candle sitting in a holder on the wall. I opened my eyes wide and stared out at the abandoned houses we were passing, the vacant stares of the people dressed in rags running by on the sidewalk, but still I saw the stone walls dripping with moisture, and heard the roar of something not entirely human. But it was the unearthly human scream of pain that finally put me over the edge.

"Shut her up!" I heard the man shout.

I could hear hysterical shrieking, not realizing it was coming from me. The sharp prick of a needle pressed into my arm, followed by blessed darkness and oblivion.

CHAPTER FOURTEEN
FEHIN

The mountain range swept backward like cresting waves into the far distance where jagged peaks rose into a sky filled with tattered charcoal clouds. There was nothing other than the foreboding landscape and the feeling of dread that came with it. Airy and I had never discussed this eventuality. When I called to her in my mind she didn't answer. She was in a completely different time line by now. There was nothing for it but to head somewhere and try and find shelter before night fell in this gods-forsaken place.

As I walked I had the distinct impression that something or someone was following me, but whenever I turned there was nothing there. I tried to keep the fear down, knowing that it would only tire me and zap what little strength I had. My arm wound was not fully healed and the food I'd eaten would soon be out of my system, leaving me weak. Water was what I needed even more than food.

My feet carried me toward the mountains in the distance, but it did not appear as though I was getting any closer. And whatever I'd felt before seemed to be closing in. When I turned this time I was sure I saw a shadow of something jump away. I called on every bit of my magic to figure out what it was, but my wizardry was gone. I stopped and turned when I felt the next prickly feeling on my arms. "Show yourselves!" I shouted. But my words were sucked away on the wind that had just come up. A moment later the wind turned into a gale and I had to hunch to keep going forward.

I trudged straight ahead, afraid to look back or forward for fear that my dread was justified—that my efforts were getting me nowhere. When I finally looked up again it did seem the range was closer, a sigh escaping my parched throat. But now night was falling in a series of strange veil-like images, each one denser than the next. They looked like sheets of rain except they were dark and dry. I could no longer see the mountains, and a moment later I could barely see my hand in front of my face. Terrified I ran off to the left, hoping to find a rock to hide behind or some place I could rest without fear of whatever was stalking me.

I was huddled on the ground when the moon appeared behind the peaks, the silvery light so welcome I almost cried out. I thought of the light beings Airy had told me about and said a mental thank you. It was then that I got a real look at the shadows that moved in and out of focus. Somehow the darkness made them visible. They circled around me like beasts circling their prey. I held up both hands. "Leave me in peace!" I shouted. They hesitated but they did not leave. "Go!" I screamed, my shriek caught and thrown back at me. The wind had returned, the beings seeming to get their energy from it as they swarmed closer, their forms shrinking and expanding, as they moved in. "No!" I held my hands over my head as they enveloped me in darkness.

I woke to the screech of a sea bird, surprised to find myself at the edge of a large body of water. How I got there was a mystery since the last thing I remembered was…before I could think about the night before a woman in a dark hooded cape sitting in front a fire took my attention. She was witch-like, hunched over the flames, gray hair hanging around a sallow face. As soon as I stirred she looked up, her dark eyes drilling into mine. "Finally," she rasped. "I thought you might sleep another day and night." She gestured. "Come share the stew I've made—it will give you much needed energy."

I pushed myself to standing and lurched toward her. I saw no pot, no sign of anything cooked or otherwise. But by the time I reached her she was holding out a steaming bowl. "Sit, eat," she said, patting the sand next to her.

Now that I was close I realized she was younger than she appeared. Her eyes held wisdom, her face not significantly lined. I took the bowl she held out and eagerly drank down the thick soup. "How did I end up here?"

She smiled. "I saved you from the 'ones who live in shadow'. They would have gobbled you up had I not come along when I did."

"What are they?"

"Shadow beings that prey on those who wander into our realm. I do not begrudge them their feasts, since they must survive in whatever manner they can, but I am glad I saved you, young wizard."

I stared at her, wondering how she knew this about me. "Is this place in the known world or are we on another planet?"

"This is what you might call a 'parallel reality'. It exists in between the moments in time. You wouldn't be here at all if it hadn't been for letting go while you were in the ether. But I'm afraid I have no way of sending you back where you belong."

"So how do I get out of here?"

She twisted her long fingers together. "I have no idea. My advice is to call out to the one who knows."

"Gunnar—or do you mean Airy?"

She stood and before I could stop her she was floating toward the sea, her black garments trailing in the sand. "Wait!" I called, heading after her, but she was already chest deep in the water and a moment later she wasn't there at all. When I turned back there was no more fire and the bowl I'd had in my hands was gone as well. Sorcery, I thought to myself. And I was glad of it-- but what now?

Gunnar if you can hear me I'm stuck in an in between place. I hope you can hear me because if you can't, I will probably die here. I scanned up and down the beach that seemed to go on forever, the sky that remained a uniform gray. The sun was somewhere but I couldn't locate it. The mountains I'd seen were far away again, the peaks just as jagged and menacing as they'd been the night before. The thought of the shadow beings made me shudder. They would come as soon as night fell. *Gunnar, please. If not for me then do it for Airy. She will be sad if I die.*

I sat on the sand and stared at the water, wondering if I should drown myself. It seemed better than being devoured by those *things.*

I was still sitting there when night fell, my pleas to Gunnar apparently falling on deaf ears. I was heading toward the water when I noticed a shape behind me. Instead of turning I ran as fast as I could, gasping as I plunged into the cold sea. The water pressed and surged as I moved forward, and then I stepped off a small embankment and went under. I tried hard not to fight it, to let the water enter my lungs and take me with it into the deeper currents, but before I could stop myself I was thrashing and sputtering to the surface. I opened my eyes to see Gunnar in the water next to me.

"If you plan to kill yourself you should probably swim out until you get tired."

I tried to laugh but all I could do was cough.

He grabbed my arm, towed me back to shore and dragged me out. "How did this happen?" he asked, looking me up and down.

"I let go of Airy before we were through—where is this place—it seems like a landscape from a dream."

"Didn't the witch explain? This is what happens when you dabble in things you don't understand. You're in a place that doesn't truly exist. It would be nearly impossible to find it again. " His dark eyes met mine. "Airy is in serious trouble, Fehin."

"So was I until you got here. Where is she?"

"Is that a round-about thank you?" he asked, before his gaze went to the horizon. When he turned back I saw the worry in his eyes, an expression he rarely had. "She's been sold. And she does not have her ring."

"But you know how to reach her, right?"

"As I have told you repeatedly, I am not authorized to—"

"And yet here you are. Why would saving her be any different?"

"Because this place is separate. Where she is, is not."

"Send me there and I'll do it."

149

He watched me for a moment. "If I do this, know that I will not be able to bail you out. But if that's what you want I will take you there."

"What happened to her ring?"

"It was taken before she went to the auction block."

"Auction block? Mr. Sand sold her."

Gunnar nodded. "Think carefully about this, Fehin. That world is—"

"I know all about it," I answered. "Who bought her?"

"You don't want to know."

"I have to know if I'm going to get her out of there. Where is she?"

"She's working in a brothel. And her ring is in Mr. Sand's possession. In order to get away you have to have the ring."

I felt sick as I pictured her. "Take me now. The sooner I get there the sooner I can free her."

"The place is north of the city in an under populated area that is very dangerous. Prostitution is not allowed and yet it flourishes in the seamier parts of the city."

"Is there a name, a way I can identify it?"

"The building is unmarked. Those who frequent it know about it."

"And it's against the law?"

Gunnar scoffed. "The authorities tend to look the other way when it comes to things of this nature."

"How do you know so much about this world?"

Gunnar frowned, his eyes dark. "I have had other dealings with the ones who run it. The inhumanity of their practices has been brought up at the council."

"The druid council?"

"Time lords, Fehin."

This was the first time I'd heard him use this term. I suddenly felt like an idiot for all my nasty comments and expectations. "I guess I understand why you can't interfere. But if I get in trouble, you—"

Gunnar shook his head. "I have been strictly prohibited and I can't afford to be thrown off the council—there's too much at stake."

"I hope I can manage," I muttered.

"I have to warn you that your magic will not work there. Just remember that in this place human life is not valued. They have cut themselves off from compassion. If you keep that in mind it will tamp down your innate empathy. You will need to be utterly ruthless. The time you've spent here is not how much time has gone by there. She's been in that place for over two months now."

I shuddered. "Airy's been working as a prostitute for all this time?"

Gunnar nodded.

CHAPTER FIFTEEN
AIRY

I had no idea how long I'd been here. My first days were so awful I'd relegated the memories to a remote part of my brain, but still I woke screaming nearly every day. Because the daytime was when I slept, the nights reserved for my job. I was given clothing, such as it was--see through lingerie that revealed nearly everything. When it was cold, shawls were provided. When my captors realized that they couldn't keep me from rebelling against my customers they began drugging me with something that dulled me down and made me forget entire swaths of time.

Although I'd performed the act I'd sworn not to many times over, I was luckier than most. My red hair gave them a reason to charge more for my services and because of this there were fewer men who could afford my price. When I did resist I was put into solitary, a room made of stone smaller than a bathroom where my claustrophobia led to panic attacks and screaming until my voice gave out. After a while I learned to tolerate the punishment, as it gave me a respite from my 'job'. In the tiny room I closed my eyes and tried to sleep, something I desperately needed.

When I wasn't in solitary I spent the days in a dorm with around a dozen other girls between the ages of thirteen and twenty-two. We talked when we could and I found out that many of them were happy with their lot. "I would be out on the plains, sure to get shot and killed if I wasn't here," one unfortunate girl told me. "I don't mind this life."

"Why do they do that?" I asked.

She stared at me in puzzlement. "What else would you do with a person who has no money, no job? They can't feed or clothe themselves. And there's a slim chance for them to get away. I've heard stories and legends regarding ones who have disappeared never to be seen again."

"You don't mind what you have to do here?" I asked, surprised.

"Why would I? It's only my body they use, not my mind. I can think whatever I want whenever I want." She smiled, pulling at a brown ringlet that had come loose from her braid.

My drugs were administered every evening before I went into the small room reserved for my business. Every night I thanked the gods for it, knowing that without it I would surely go insane. As it was, not every man who visited me wanted to have sex. There were a few who merely wanted to talk, and spent the hour complaining about this and that, giving me a glimpse into a rigid caste system. Men and women married and had children, but if they didn't have enough means the children were taken away and put to work in factories.

Unfortunately there were others who had no regard for anything other than their pleasure. It was after they were there that I cried myself to sleep. They were the ones who often drove me to shriek, bringing the matron running.

Between sessions the matron always came in to clean me up and straighten the bedclothes in preparation for the next customer. And if I'd succumbed to tears she slapped me across the face. "You'd better wipe those tears from your eyes," she told me harshly. "If I catch you crying during a session you know what happens."

"How do you know if I'm crying? Do the men tell you?"

"Don't be silly, girl. I watch." She laughed nastily.

It was then that I noticed the small mirror that hung over the bed.

I thought about what my friend had said: *It's only my body they use, not my mind.* I wished I could separate the two.

Each day seemed to drag into the next, my mind becoming dulled and disinterested. I lost weight and wondered how I could be attractive to the opposite sex, but still they came for me because of my hair. The owners, Renz and Chaz Langdon, fed me intravenously from time to time, trying to keep up my strength—after all, I was their prize possession.

"Now, Airy," Renz said gently on one of her visits. "You must not starve yourself, dear. Think about life as a runner. Being maimed by an arrow and dying slowly out there is a lot worse than your life here where you're well fed, have a place to sleep and friends to talk to. Try to keep that in mind when you refuse to eat."

I knew the threat implied was real. If I got too thin I would be taken out there and turned loose. I had the feeling I wouldn't last very long.

In the early mornings before I fell asleep my mind would turn to Fehin, wondering where he was. Even if he found me now I doubted he could ever love me again. My body had been used up, my mind as empty as the hazy sky, when I managed to catch a glimpse of it. All the windows were blacked out as though to hide this building from prying eyes. What went on in here was against the law, not that that stopped it from continuing.

The one time I'd been allowed out of the building was for a 'showing'. It was during an award ceremony in the square held for the hunter with the most prowess. Before the festivities began the Landons paraded me in front of the crowds in my transparent finery, hoping to bring in more business. It shamed me to be there, my mind shutting down as I tried to shut out the jeers and catcalls, the wolf whistles that rang in my ears.

What I saw that day turned my stomach and made me more aware than ever of the evil that went on in Canhavu. A man had been killed—a runner. And his body was displayed for all to see, the crossbow bolt still embedded in his chest. He was young, his muscles taut and sinewy from his time in the 'wild'. His brown eyes were still open, the look in them that of a wild animal. The clapping for the indigo who brought him down was deafening. The killer bowed and smiled, standing next to his 'kill' like a king.

Later I asked the girls in the dorm what it was all about.

"It is the only way for an indigo to move up," one of them told me. "Killing a man or woman who has eluded hunters for a certain length of time will allow the hunter to join the next class up."

"What is there to eat out there—how do the runners stay alive?"

"That's what the sport is all about. The runners who find the nuts and fruit and water placed here and there are the ones who survive. The others are easy to kill because they are weak and dehydrated. Those kills do nothing for the indigos who shoot them."

"How do they know which ones are the prize catch?"

"There is a board in the square with the descriptions, how long they've been out there, and where they've been sighted."

No wonder we saw so many indigos heading out with crossbows that first day. And now I knew what the caches of nuts and water were all about.

Once every thirty days the prostitutes had an appointment with the doctor to make sure we didn't have infections, and to renew our once a month birth control shot. Dr. Radnor was a kind woman in her forties who did her job efficiently and well. "Use the douche every day," she told me on her last visit. "It will burn, but it will help with pain and with infection." She looked me over critically. "You need to eat, Airy. If you don't you will succumb to one of the many diseases that run rampant through the city. The men you see have surely been exposed."

"Maybe if I'm sick I won't have to perform."

She shook her head, her eyes dark. "I wouldn't count on it. The Langdon's are in this for the money. Girls with infections have been turned out to run with the hunted. Be careful," she warned.

I had noticed a few girls disappearing and wondered what had happened to them. Now I knew.

Most men who frequented the brothel were the ones like Mr. Sand or others a step down, who wore the bright clothing. Magistrates like Mr. Sand were high in the political system of the country and nearly above the law, the others who wore the bright clothes still subject to the police, but held in high esteem--if caught for disobeying a law or two a few coins could make things right.

I was shocked the day Mr. Sand appeared asking for me. When I took him into the small room where I conducted my business I hoped he had come to talk, but that wish was immediately dashed when I saw the eager look in his piggy eyes. "What is the government here?" I asked, trying to forestall the inevitable.

He looked up from where he was unbuttoning his pants. "Seven magistrates own fifty one percent or more of the seven businesses in Canhavu. I happen to be one of them—we are in charge of things here."

"What are the companies and which one is yours?"

He ticked them off on his fingers. "Horses, hunting paraphernalia, drugs, health clinics, brothel, clothing and carts. I am part owner in the company that manufactures crossbows. As you can imagine it is very lucrative."

"What about other food—don't people grow vegetables?"

His expression changed to one of irritation. "Enough questions, girl. You are a delectable little morsel and I want a taste of it before you wear out."

When he took hold of my arm I let out a piercing shriek and kept on screaming until the matron came running. "I'm so sorry, Mr. Sand," she said, dragging me roughly from the room. "What do you mean by this behavior?" she hissed. "Mr. Sand is a magistrate—he could turn you into a runner, and I hope he does. I'm sick to death of dealing with your outbursts. This time you'll be down there until you can show some respect." She pulled me by the arm down the rickety stairs and shoved me into the tiny stone prison where I fell on my knees, bruising them in the process. The light went out and I was left in darkness.

Time went by, my mind playing tricks on me. I had no water, no food, and the only way to relieve myself was to do it on the floor behind me. My prison had no air circulation and began to stink, my belly pulling in on itself as the days went by. Because I was sure it was days and not hours. I had never been left this long. Was I destined to die here? I wondered if Mr. Sand had given the order.

I began to dream, first of Fehin when we first met, and then of Otherworld when I was a young girl playing with the wolves in the sunlit meadows. But then a darkness seemed to come over my consciousness, bringing with it scenes from what I'd been doing here, the faces of the men parading by and taunting me. They were in here with me, their fingers pulling at my skin, groping me in the dark. I screamed and screamed, but no one came.

And when I couldn't scream anymore I curled up in a ball, whimpering as my rational mind seemed to drift away. I was an animal now, my only thought to escape. I hardly felt the pain as I scrabbled at the stone with my nails until I couldn't lift my arms. I had to have water. A world of night sucked me down, creatures clawing at me as I tried to get away. I rolled away from them only to find others taking their place. I screamed but no sound came out of my mouth.

CHAPTER SIXTEEN
FEHIN

It was night when Gunnar left me on a side street inside the city. "Here is the address of a man who will tattoo your arm. Once it's done you'll be in the system."

"What about money, clothing?"

"Jem will give you clothing and enough money to keep you out of jail. But you'd better get your business done and get out of here quickly." He handed me a pistol and an eight-inch hunting knife. "On market day you'll see the ships that come up the river. That's the best time to get Airy away since a lot of the patrons and the owners will be busy in town. It only happens once a month and the goods are much needed."

"What kind of goods?"

"Things they don't have here like horse fodder, drugs, clothing for the masses. Foodstuffs for the wealthy and alcohol are on the list as well."

"How is it paid for?"

"Trade mostly—metal items and slaves."

"How big is this place—where is it?"

Gunnar shook his head. "It's in the future. To be honest I'm unclear as to how you and Airy reached it."

"I wish we hadn't," I muttered.

"Strap the gun on under your shirt and stow the knife in your boot. The people here don't have guns but they do have crossbows, bows and arrows, and knives. If you must use the gun know that the report will alert others to your presence here."

"One more thing. How do I find this Jem's house?"

Gunnar handed over a small piece of paper. "I drew a map. This dot here is where we are." His finger traced along a zigzag line. "This dot here is where Jem lives. Make sure you arrive before dawn and leave after dusk. It will be safer that way."

"And will Jem know how to get to the brothel?"

Gunnar nodded, looking around. "I've got to go. Good luck." A second later he was gone.

I looked up at the walls of black stone that turned into a fine silvery metal ten feet above the ground. How these people had managed to build these enormous structures was anyone's guess. It seemed they had little in the way of natural resources. Had the ships brought all the materials from across the sea or did they have mines here? I stared at the map using the small penlight Gunnar had given me. Jem's house was at least five miles from here, and already the horizon was lightening. I hurried out of my hiding place and made haste along the deserted street.

"Who did you say you were?" Suspicious blue eyes peered at me from a narrow face surrounded with shoulder-length white hair.

"I'm Fehin. Gunnar sent me."

"Oh, Gunnar. Of course." He scanned up and down the street. "Come in quickly."

Once I stepped over the threshold he shut the door and locked and bolted it from the inside. "One can't be too careful," he mumbled before looking up at me.

He led me past two ordinary front rooms before pulling back a Persian looking tapestry at the end of the hall revealing a padlocked metal door. Producing a key from around his neck he opened it and swung it inward. "Please," he said, gesturing for me to go ahead. I stared into darkness wondering if he would shut me up in here. No one would ever my screams through a door that thick.

He chuckled, seeming to recognize my trepidation. "Don't worry. Any friend of Gunnar's is a friend of mine." He reached around to flip on the light and followed me inside before pulling the door shut behind us. "It locks automatically," he said, pointing to the keyhole on the inside.

It looked like a mad scientist's laboratory with tubing and beakers on a metal tray next to a cot, clothing stacked on shelves, boxes of drugs on another. Heavy locked metal boxes were stacked on top of each other on another shelf. On another metal table I saw tattooing tools and inks, stacked white cloths.

"Are you armed, Fehin?"

I nodded, pulling back my shirt to reveal the gun.

"I hope Gunnar warned you about shooting here in the city. We do not have guns here, a constant source of irritation to those who like to hunt. There's been some talk of trading with the Chinese, but so far no deal has been struck. But if anyone finds out you have a gun you will be killed for it. These people here are ruthless."

Ruthless. The same word Gunnar had used to describe how I needed to be. "I'll only use it in an emergency. I came here to rescue my girlfriend. She's being held at the bordello."

"Held or working?" Jem asked.

"I figure she's working, but I'm sure she isn't happy about it."

Jem shook his head. "It is a very nasty place. The prostitutes are not treated well. The sooner you get her out of there the better. But I must warn you it will not be easy." He pointed to the table. "Let's get to work on your tattoo. Without it the authorities will pick you up and either turn you loose on the plain or sell you." He glanced at the small window that revealed the coming dawn. "I suggest you sleep here once it turns light and head out after it's dark again. That way your tattoo will have time to heal and you'll be rested and fed."

I pushed myself up to sit on the table and rolled up my sleeve. "Will it hurt?"

"Not too much," he said, rubbing alcohol along my inner wrist.

The process was slow and painful, blood pooling on my skin as he pressed ink into the numbers he created. I tried to ignore it, my mind going to Airy. Several times I called out to her in my mind, but I got no response. Was she even still alive? "What if one of the girls gets sick?" I asked at one point.

He glanced up from his work. "If the condition is untreatable they are released into the wild. This also goes for gonorrhea and other sexually transmitted diseases. The owners can't afford to have sick girls."

"Is there only one bordello in town?"

"One large one and several satellite facilities. Do you know where she is?"

"No. I assume she's at the big one."

He let out a sigh, bending to what he was doing. "The place is like a fortress, Fehin. I would suggest going in as a customer. That way you can get the lay of the land." He straightened and wiped sweat from his forehead. "Finished. Now I have to input it into the system. You will soon be a member of Canhavu society, such as it is." He moved to a computer and began typing.

"Where do the electronics come from?"

"Our friends across the sea provide them. We do have an electronic system here for using them; unfortunately individual machines are not secure. I've had to jury-rig this thing to keep my work secret."

"So you're basically in the resistance?"

Jem laughed. "I suppose you could call it that. There are only a handful of us. The risks are too great for most people."

"Why don't you leave?"

He turned from the computer. "The only way I could leave is to stow away on one of the ships. And from what I understand things are not any better anywhere else." "Do you know the year?"

"As far as I've heard it's 2567, but time is of no importance here."

"What is important?"

"Staying alive."

"But why would you even want to in a place like this? I think I'd take my chances on the boat."

"I have friends here, Fehin. And Gunnar needs me to do my job. I'm an important cog in the wheel of this place, bad as it is."

After Jem made eggs and we ate he showed me into a small bedroom with no windows. "Sleep here. When it's dark again I'll wake you."

I lay there thinking for a long time, but finally my lack of rest and frayed nerves got the best of me and I fell into a dreamless sleep.

∽

"Fehin."

I woke immediately and sat up, staring at Jem backlit in the doorway. "Is it night already?"

An hour later I was dressed in an outlandish jacket and loose-fitting trousers of reds and purples, a hat stuck on my head. "Why not the indigo?" I asked, looking at the shelf.

"The indigos are not rich enough to afford a prostitute. Now listen carefully. Your name is Silas Bret and you have a small import business. You sell beads and shells and other baubles in the market." He handed me a small pouch. "There is enough money here to purchase the most expensive whore and still have some left over."

"Where is the bordello?"

"It will take you several hours on foot. The good thing is they stay open until dawn. Does anyone know you?"

"Only Mr. Sand."

"Ah, Mr. Sand—a nasty piece of work. He does frequent the bordello but you'll have to take your chances. You look quite different in this get-up."

I stared into the mirror on the wall, surprised by what I saw. My hair tied back emphasized my cheekbones, my eyes dark and brooding. The colors did something to my skin, casting a sort of greenish tinge across it. "I hardly recognize myself."

Jem smiled. "That's the entire point." He held out a map of the city. "We are here and this is the brothel," he said, showing me the main roads that ran between. "You need to follow the line of buildings as far as you can and stay out of sight. Once you reach the factory section it isn't far. It's a green metal building set back from the road. Over the door you'll see a sign that says Factory # 1. Knock on the door and introduce yourself. Tell them you've heard of a prostitute named—what is her name?"

"Airy."

"Tell them you've heard of Airy and wanted to sample her for yourself."

I grimaced.

"Sorry, Fehin, but this is life here. You have to deal with it as it is or you'll be dead before you even reach her."

He led the way to the front door. "If you run into trouble don't hesitate to use your knife. Save the firearm for emergencies only." He unlocked the door. "Good luck."

I turned to thank him but the door had already closed. I heard the sound of the bolt sliding across. I patted the gun and my pocket where my moneybag rested, and headed into the darkness.

The warren of roads in the middle of the city had me going in circles. It seemed that this was where the original town had been, filled with ancient houses and many other dilapidated four-story buildings constructed out of wood.

They had been added onto over the years, rooms leaning precariously out over the narrow roadway and several porches on some that seemed not to go with the original designs. The area was dense, connecting walls going for blocks before a break and another line of housing on the other side of a narrow alleyway. No wonder they ran out of trees. The roads were narrow and curved, taking me further and further away from where I needed to be. Lights hung in doorways leading into tiny restaurants and possibly gambling dens that reminded me of what it must be like in China.

In an alley I was accosted by a punk kid and had to use my knife, realizing too late that he was only about ten years old. And now he lay dead in a pool of his own blood. I felt sick as I hurried away.

By the time dawn broke I was still wandering lost in the city. And before I knew it the hustle and bustle of commerce had begun. I walked the sidewalks with the others dressed like myself, watching the indigos skulking and trying to stay out of the line of sight. Businesses were being opened, some with food, others for coffee, or something that smelled like coffee. I was hungry but I dared not stop for fear of giving myself away. But after an hour of this I decided to use a few of my coins to buy some breakfast.

A long counter ran along one wall and behind it waitresses dressed in black uniforms scurried, bringing plates of food and drink to those seated on the other side. I took my place at one end and tried to see how much people were paying for things. It seemed that one gold coin, similar to the one Airy found in the woods, was enough for a cup of coffee and a plate of something that resembled eggs. When the waitress came to take my order I pointed to the person seated two stools down. "I'll have what he's having."

She nodded and bustled off. When she brought my plate I handed her one coin, which she took without batting an eye. So far so good.

The drink she left resembled coffee but wasn't. I drank it anyway. The eggs tasted like powdered eggs but I was hungry and ate them all. "Do you sell water?" I asked the waitress when she came by. Her eyes widened and I knew this was not the right question to ask. "I mean where do I get a drink?"

She seemed to relax. "The town square has water." She turned and hurried off.

I left shortly after that, my mind on what I would do from now until it got dark again. First thing was to head to the square and get a drink of water. I followed a line of people dressed as I was, hoping this was also their destination. Water was not served with food here.

I saw it in the distance, a place where people did their business and stopped to chat. There were stone benches and a strange sort of monument in the center depicting a man dressed as I was, holding a bow and arrow and chasing another man who was naked. **The hunt** was engraved on a metal plaque at the bottom.

There were no indigos present in the square and I wondered why. Along the edges I spied several places where water had collected in bowls made of stone. I headed toward one, hoping there wasn't disease present in the standing water that looked none too clean. I watched to see how others drank before bending down to scoop it into my mouth. When I'd had my fill of the foul tasting liquid I found a bench and sat down, hoping to pass the next hours without incident. But when a man sat next to me I realized this was not to be.

"Who are you and what is your business here?" he asked, his beady eyes suspicious.

Did I look that different? "I'm Silas Bret. I'm in imports—beads and such," I answered, trying to copy his manner of speech.

"I have not seen you here before, nor have I seen you down by the docks. Why is that?"

My hands went into fists. "I must be there at different times than you. And as far as the square, I try to avoid the crowds." I looked him straight in the eye trying to employ some of my wizardry to get him to back off.

It seemed to work, his gaze moving to some other unsuspecting victim who looked somewhat out of place. "Well, good to meet you, Mr. Bret. Perhaps we will meet again." He rose and headed toward the bewildered looking man standing at the edge of the square. I decided that the safest thing for me was to find my way to the brothel and wait until it opened again.

I was on a side street close to the factory district when I saw a group of young men dressed in indigo. They were eyeing me, and all of a sudden I realized I was alone in an area where people of my station did not venture unless going to someplace like the brothel. But the brothel wasn't open yet. I could feel their animosity, the gleam in their eyes as they circled me like animals. I put my hand up, attempting to employ magic to stop them, but when it didn't work my hand went to the gun. And when they all rushed in at once I fired. I hit one and fired again, hitting another before the rest turned and fled. But the sound had not gone unnoticed and a minute later a man dressed in a uniform approached me.

"Where did you get the firearm?" he asked, his keen gaze on the gun still in my hand.

"I traded for it," I lied. "I'm in import/export and it came with my last shipment."

He surveyed the two men I'd killed, his gaze impassive. They were very dead, blood turning the indigo fabric black where they lay sprawled. "You must be aware that guns are not allowed here. And killing the way you just did is also not allowed. Only hunting is allowed and that is done with other weaponry. I am afraid I will have to confiscate your weapon and take you in." He held out his hand.

I placed the gun in his palm knowing full well that it would be his prize. Instead of cuffing me as I'd expected, he held my arm, leading the way down the street toward his waiting conveyance pulled by a skinny horse. I couldn't get rid of the sight of those two men I'd killed. I'd never killed anyone in my life and now I had three murders on my conscience. One of them was a kid and none were armed. What had I become?

After confiscating my knife the cop ushered me into a cell with two other men. The cell door banged closed behind me, the cop locking it before walking away. As soon as the cop was out of sight the two men dressed in indigo sitting on a bench in the back rose and came toward me. I put up my fists, but they were burly and angry and my feeble attempts to fight back were nothing compared to how they fought. They knew exactly where to land the punches, working off of each other as they took me down. I realized there was nothing I could do but let them beat the shit out of me. Maybe it would relieve my conscience, I thought, just before I blacked out.

Jem somehow became aware of what had happened, appearing in late afternoon to bail me out. "You have to watch it with these guys," he said as we left the police station. "They enjoy pinning something on the class above them. And the gun issue is a big one. I tried but they wouldn't release it back to you. At least I got your knife," he said, handing it to me.

I stuck it in my boot. "I figured as much. The cop, or whatever you call them here, lusted after that gun. But now I'm down to a knife, and from what I've seen so far there's no lack of violence here."

"It seems you got your share of it while you were inside," he said wryly, glancing at my bruised and battered face. "You're going to have a major black eye and I hope they didn't crack a bone."

I ran my fingers gingerly across my face. "Nothing's broken. But I might have a cracked rib."

He shook his head, his lips pressing together. "Hopefully you'll be off the streets and with Airy in an hour or so. But I wouldn't attempt any rescue until you have a clear idea of how to do it."

"At least I know I won't be shot."

Jem scoffed. "Just bludgeoned to death, knifed, or shot with a crossbow."

I laughed. "I guess this is where we part ways. Thanks, Jem. Without you, I—"

He waved his hand dismissively. "That's what I'm here for. Do you know your way back to the brothel?"

"I think so. I paid close attention when we were driving to the police station."

"Good." With that statement he turned and walked quickly away.

Two hours later I was slamming my fist against the metal door. I'd been at it for more than five straight minutes before it finally opened revealing a very annoyed middle-aged woman. "Do you have an appointment?" she asked in an irritated tone.

"Well no, but I heard about this gal with red hair and—"

"Sorry. She's booked. If you want her you'll have to schedule with me. My soonest appointment is not until tomorrow night, and there is only one slot at ten." She held out her hand.

"You want me to pay now?"

"Yes. That will insure your appointment."

I dug into my bag. "How much?"

She glanced at the bag. "How much do you have?"

I grabbed a handful of coins and held them out.

"That is not nearly enough. This girl is very popular."

I pulled out another handful realizing that it was nearly all I had. She took them, counting it up before stashing the coins in her pocket. "When you come back go the other entrance and tell the person who answers the door that you've paid already."

"What if he or she doesn't believe me?"

"Say you've come for Airy. That will get you in. No one knows her name unless they've booked ahead."

I felt sick imagining what Airy was going through. I had to get her out of here. "Thanks. I'll be back tomorrow night."

She slammed the door and I heard the lock click.

What in hell was I going to do for the rest of the night and all day tomorrow? I walked around the building, checking for open windows or possible escape routes, but what I saw did not look promising. Bars covered any windows there were, and the rest of the building was locked up tight. A back door with a red light above it was the only other entrance, and when I approached it a warning sound went off, stopping when I backed away. This was the entrance to let me in? Maybe they had some system for appointments and there weren't any right now. Whatever it was I wished I had the damn gun.

I slept in an alley, curled up in a doorway to an abandoned building. Or at least I hoped it was abandoned. Down here it was hard to tell. I heard rats in the night, hoping they wouldn't think I was dead and try for a nibble. By the time morning came I was stiff and sore, not to mention tired from a night of fitful sleep. I was stretching, trying to get the kinks out of my neck and back, when I heard the unmistakable sound of a ship's bellowing horn. The dock was close. Checking out the ship would be a good diversion for the hours I had to fill until night.

I found the docks purely by my keen sense of smell. The coal, or whatever they burned, mixed with the stench of garbage led me directly to where the enormous vessel had docked. The place was teeming with humanity, sweating men lifting barrels and boxes down to indigos who hurried to load them on carts, horses straining as they left the docks pulling their heavy loads. The cacophony of many languages came to my ears as I stood in the shadows trying to make sense of what was going on. A few moments later two large carts appeared, filled with naked men and women. There were twelve of them tied together and I watched the deckhands lead them onto the ship and away. The expressions on their faces would stick in my memory—as though there was no more hope at all.

Men in dark trousers and long black coats with cravats at their throats, and women in dresses with bustles and feathery hats that could have come from the eighteen-hundreds moved gracefully down the gangplank. They all looked Asian and seemed genteel and wealthy, meeting up with officials who escorted them to the fancy motor driven waiting conveyances.

Once they departed I made my way up the gangplank hoping to get a better idea of what was going on. But once on the ship I came face to face with a Chinese man who did not appear at all friendly. "State your business," he said, his hard eyes on mine.

"How much does it cost to travel to China?" I asked.

He looked me over, a frown appearing over his narrowed eyes. "You do not have enough," he told me. "We take only the magistrates."

"But I just saw all those men and women loaded. What about them?"

He stared at me. "You want to be slave?"

"Of course not. I'm a business owner, I have the right to—"

He shook his head, his pigtail swinging. "You have no rights in China, and now I suggest you get off my ship before I alert the authorities."

"What about the passengers? Will they stay here long?"

"They conduct business and leave on the outgoing tide. We trade with Canhavu, nothing more."

When I turned to leave his heavy hand came down on my shoulder. "Do not think about stowing away. The ones who do so are thrown overboard." He let out a nasty laugh.

I didn't turn as I headed down the gangplank with as much dignity as I could muster. It wouldn't look good for me to appear afraid, although my heart was beating a staccato rhythm. There was something very unsettling about what was going on here. It seemed that China was just as bad as Canhavu, and maybe worse.

CHAPTER SEVENTEEN
AIRY

I felt my body being lifted, the sound of mumbled conversation. "Better throw her in the tub before we take her back to the room. She's got shit all over her."

Someone laughed. "Room is too small to get away from it."

"Renz is going to be angry we left her there for so long. She may not come out of it. Look at her—she's barely breathing."

"I told you we needed to give her more than water. She's nothing but skin and bone now. I'm not taking responsibility for this, Cree."

"It was your idea to leave her there for a week, not mine. If I hadn't gone into that cesspool and poured water down her throat a couple of times she'd be dead now. Which one of us is going to tell Renz how bad off she is?"

I heard the sound of water splashing and a second later the cold hit me like a shock. I screamed and came fully awake.

"That did it," the matron said, looking down on me. She scrubbed me with something rough that left red welts all over my skin. "You are disgusting, girl." When she pushed me under I gagged and took water into my lungs, sputtering as I pushed upward.

"Don't kill her, Cree. Renz will have your neck if you do her in," the male companion said, chuckling.

"I'm glad Renz had to take that trip. She won't have any idea how long we left her there."

"Come, Airy," Renz said, sitting on my bed. "Time for your shot."

I looked at her, barely able to keep her face in focus. I felt the prick of the needle and the blessed languor come over me, blocking out everything. I closed my eyes.

"Airy? It's time to go to work." She pulled me to sitting and took hold of one of my hands where the nails had been torn off. "What has happened to you? Cree?" I heard her shout. "What's wrong with Airy? What happened to her nails?"

"I don't know Ma'am. Maybe she's sick?"

"How many appointments does she have tonight?"

"At least five, Ma'am."

"Take her to her room and see if she comes out of it. If she doesn't, come and get me."

Renz left and the matron pulled me to standing. "If you breathe a word of what we did you'll be very sorry," she hissed, dragging me out the door.

I was lying on the bed when I heard the lock click, the sound of a man's footsteps entering the space. I tried to move but couldn't.

A hand came down on my arm. "Airy?"

I opened my eyes and flinched away, unable to say a word.

Fehin's eyes filled with tears. "I came to get you out of here."

This was a dream—it had to be. I was still in the dark hole. I gasped and closed my eyes.

"I'm a paying customer," I heard him whisper.

What cruel joke was this--Fehin here as a customer?

"And I plan to save you whether you want me to or not," he continued.

I began to shake, my body convulsing as the room closed in. When he put his arms around me I let out a moan. "I'm not..." I managed before my throat closed up.

"I don't care what you've done. I've killed three men."

He sat on his haunches next to the bed and stared at me. "Tell me about this place. How can I get you out of here? What happened to the ring?"

"Mr. Sand..."

"Mr. Sand has your ring?"

I managed to nod before closing my eyes against the bright overhead light.

I heard a click and the door opened. "Is everything all right in here?"

"Everything's fine," Fehin said, his fingers grasping mine. The door closed.

"Airy, you're cold as ice. And you're emaciated. What are they doing to you?" He looked down at my hand. "What happened to your nails? You need to have these treated—they could be infected."

"Dr. Radnor," I managed to croak before darkness fell over me.

"I swear I'll get you out of here. I don't care if I have to kill every last one of them!" I heard him shout as I drifted away.

When I woke Dr. Radnor was next to my bed. "What did they do to you, Airy? Can you tell me?"

I shook my head and closed my eyes, feeling a prick in my arm.

"I've given you a stimulant to wake you out of this…whatever this state is. Something happened to you and I plan to find out what. You are in no condition to work and I'm not afraid to tell the Langdons.

I felt a little jolt, my body suddenly coming alive. I sat up.

"That's better. Now tell me what happened. I have to know so I can help you."

"They left me too long in the room."

"The room—ah yes, solitary confinement." She peered at me. "How long, Airy?"

I shrugged. "A week, I think I heard them say."

"An entire week with no food, no light and barely any water, from the look of it. And from what I understand you're claustrophobic. Is that correct? Did you try and scratch your way out?" she asked, gently picking up my right hand. She shook her head as she examined the shredded nails and the open and bleeding beds where the nails had come off. "Who did this to you? I'm sure it wasn't Renz. She would never let her cash cow be out of commission for that long."

I nodded toward the door.

"Cree."

"I…" I choked and coughed.

"You haven't been able to utter a word for several days now. That's trauma, Airy. Have they kept you working?"

I shook my head, no. "Fehin, my boyfriend was here," I whispered. I began to shake and wrapped my arms around myself.

"Your body is in shock. I am going to the authorities this time. I can't stand idly by and let them get away with this."

"Please hurry," I whispered through chattering teeth.

"The drug will wear off in an hour or so. Hopefully I'll be back by the end of the day. Sit tight, Airy. I'll get you out of here."

I was asleep when I heard shouting, doors slamming and arguing. Not long after that the door to my room was yanked open. I expected to see Cree but instead it was a woman in a uniform. "Are you Airy?"

"Yes," I managed to say.

"You're coming with me."

I stood shakily and followed her out the door and down the hall. We rode together on a freight elevator down to the first floor. Once we were outside she handed me a blanket that I wrapped around my half naked shivering body.

"Thank you," I heard Dr. Radnor say. And then I saw Fehin.

"She is bought and paid for," Fehin told the policewoman as she came forward. His eyes met mine. "And I won't hurt her like the Langdons did."

"Bought and paid for means nothing in these circumstances," the policewoman said, glancing at the doctor. "The Langdons have been accused by a higher-up and they will stand trial."

Dr. Radnor came toward me. "Airy, you are the reason I had the courage to report this. I've been working for them for five years now and never have I seen someone hurt as much as you. It will take a long time for you to heal." She glanced at Fehin. "But I can see this man loves you and will take good care of you. I hope you can put all this behind you."

Behind me the raid was in full swing, bewildered girls dressed in skimpy lingerie being brought out, guards being hand-cuffed. Dr. Radnor obviously had a lot of pull with the authorities. In the meantime Fehin had hold of my arm and was leading me down the street. Once we rounded the corner I jerked away from him and ran, my only thought to get as far away as I could.

"Airy! Airy!" I heard him yell. I kept going, rounding corners until I arrived at a dead end. I couldn't let him see me like this. Tears filled my eyes.

"Why did you do that?" he asked gently. "Why would you run from me?"

I shook my head, sniffling. "Don't look at me," I pleaded.

He tipped my face up. "I love you, Airy."

I wrenched away. "No you don't. You love the person I was." I looked up at him then. "I'm not that person anymore."

He looked about to cry. "You'll heal, Airy. I know how you must feel but—"

"No, you don't."

He pulled me to my feet and led the way back. Once we reached the main street he said, "Act like you don't know me."

I didn't have to act like anything—I wasn't the Airy he knew and what memories I had of him had long since been eliminated from my brain. All I could see was the room, remembering the stench and the hours of darkness and terror. The blinding thirst that caused me to scrabble like an animal at the unforgiving stone. The part of me that was Airy was long gone.

CHAPTER EIGHTEEN
FEHIN

If Airy hadn't mentioned Dr. Radnor's name this rescue never would have happened. Luckily with Jem's support I was able to locate the doc and enlist her help. I told her who I was, but left the part out about being from another time. She was primed for my account. She had friends in high places, she assured me. "Meet me tomorrow at the brothel," she'd said. I didn't know what time so I waited in the shadows until she arrived with the police.

I knew from my brief talk with Dr. Radnor that something truly horrible had happened to Airy, but I didn't know details. "She will need a lot of tender care, both mentally and physically," the doctor said before Airy was brought out. I was just about to question her when Airy emerged from the building. When she saw me she barely acknowledged my existence.

When I took hold of her hand she balked like a skittish young horse and pulled away. "Airy, you have to come with me," I told her. "I won't hurt you, I promise."

The look in her eyes was one I'd never seen before and I wondered if she'd been driven insane. She certainly looked the part. "Do you have any idea how to get your ring back?" I asked as I virtually dragged her along the sidewalk.

She shook her head, her expression blank. It was then that she jerked away from me. I ran after her down one street and up another until she came to a place where she was trapped. When I tried to talk to her it was like she didn't know me, her eyes like that of a wild animal.

Once I got her back to the main street I hailed a conveyance and gave them Jem's address. There was no other place for us to go and getting out of here without the ring was impossible.

Jem answered the door, his eyes going wide when he saw Airy. "What have they done to her?" he whispered.

"I don't know because she won't talk."

Jem led the way to an extra room, gesturing for us to go in, but as soon as the door closed Airy began to scream, and she didn't stop until I opened the door. "Afraid of being locked in," I said to Jem who watched her. I left the door open and went with Jem, hoping to have a private word. I needn't have worried since Airy seemed barely aware of anything around her, her dull gaze on the floor next to where she stood.

"I'm going to need Gunnar," I told Jem. "Airy has a ring that can take us through time, but Mr. Sand has it."

"I don't know what to tell you. Mr. Sand is protected, and as far as breaking into his place I doubt you could without knowing a person on the inside."

I thought of the maid, wishing she hadn't been killed in Milltown. "Every time I'm in public I run the risk of being found out."

"If the ring belongs to Airy maybe she can use some ploy to get it from Mr. Sand."

I grimaced. "Have you taken a hard look at her? She probably doesn't even remember she had a ring." I shook my head and stared into the distance. A second later I heard a thump and turned to see Airy crumpled on the floor. I hurried to her and felt for a pulse. "Jem, she's not breathing!" I did CPR, finally getting her to breathe, but when she opened her eyes they were terrified, as though she'd never seen me before. She made a little mewling noise and tried to move away. "Airy, it's me, Fehin. I'm not going to hurt you."

I waited for her to get up, trying as hard as I could not to help. When she was standing I pointed toward the bed. "Rest. And when you wake you can have a bite to eat."

She sank onto the bed, her wary gaze on me. When I left the room she turned on her side and closed her eyes.

"Jesus," I muttered. "What am I going to do?"

"We have to call Gunnar. This is an emergency," Jem answered.

Between Jem and myself we managed to spoon feed Airy, but she fought us every time, and the amount of food we got into her was negligible. Nearly every night she woke screaming, bringing me running from where I slept on the couch. But any attempts I made to console her were met with terrified stares. I worried for her sanity.

"Have you called to Gunnar? Because I've been trying to reach him every day for two weeks," I told Jem after another session of trying to get food into Airy. We left her curled up on the bed and went into the computer room.

"I've been trying to reach him too. This is not like him, especially in a situation like this."

"What if we stow away on the boat? At least in China I could get her some help."

"Why do you think that? I have no idea what life is like there, but I doubt it's much better than here."

"I'll take my chances since they used to have amazing acupuncture and herbal medicine. Airy needs more than you or I can give her."

"And you think you can keep that crazed girl quiet as a stowaway?"

I sighed thinking about the warning about being thrown overboard. "Drugs. You need to get me some drugs."

Jem shook his head, frowning. "This is dangerous, Fehin. If you get caught I won't be able to bail you out. The punishment for trying to leave here is death by hunting. Do you understand?"

"And the punishment if they find us on the boat is to throw us overboard," I said.

"How do you know that?"

"I talked with a worker on the ship that came in a few days ago."

His eyes widened. "You have a lot of balls, Fehin. You could have been killed on the spot!"

"I have to do something. I don't see her coming out of this without psychological help. Do you have therapy here?"

Jem scoffed. "What do you think? The ship arrives again in less than a month. If we haven't heard from Gunnar by then I'll find you some drugs. I wish there was another way, though. The odds for success are not good with this particular plan."

"What are the odds, do you think?"

Jem laughed. "I'd say under one percent that you make it to China."

"How long a trip is it?"

"Eight to ten days unless they stop at another port."

We spent the rest of the afternoon talking about the layout of the ship and possible hiding places. "You have to have food and water along and be in an area where no one ever goes--a tall order. And when in hell you could get on board without someone seeing you is another matter."

"Tell me what the city is like. Have you been there?"

Jem shook his head. "I have friends that have, though."

It seemed that the city of Shanghai where the boat would dock was a sprawling mass of humanity. Not too different from what I knew from reading about it at college. I could get lost in a place like that, a good thing if I had money and could get Airy the help she needed.

"Many speak English there," Jem told me, "but the culture is just as violent as this one, including the caste system we have here in Canhavu. The only saving grace, from what I've heard from the merchants, is the medical system, for lack of a better description, and the food. They have rain there and water to irrigate the fields of rice and other plants they grow."

"I need to earn some money before the boat comes back."

"People of your station don't work, Fehin. The only way you can get work is as an indigo."

"Well then, I'll be an indigo."

"It isn't that simple. The numbers on your wrist are for a different class. I can't erase them. I have money saved up but it won't be enough."

"I'm sorry, Jem. You've done so much for us already. I think I'm going a little crazy myself. Let's just hope that Gunnar comes through. How in hell did Airy take us so far into the future? Our plan was to go to the past."

Jem shrugged. "Maybe the ring has a mind of its own."

"I wish I had that damn ring," I muttered.

"Maybe you should try to steal it back. Stowing away seems way more risky than breaking into Mr. Sand's house."

"You think so?" I asked hopefully.

Jem pressed his lips together. "It's a bloodbath either way," he said, pushing the hair back from his lined face. "You'll need to watch the house and see what Mr. Sand's schedule is like. If you can get a bead on that, maybe there's a slim chance."

CHAPTER NINETEEN
AIRY

I felt like I was surrounded with a thick substance, filling my brain with fog and not allowing me to think. When I was awake all I could see was the parade of men I'd serviced, their hard eyes following me. When I slept I dreamed of the room and the horror of the nightmares and the feeling of suffocating. That was when I'd wake screaming. And the man who came to help me was barely recognizable, as though he'd been one of my johns instead of the person I used to love.

I tried really hard to lift myself out of the numbness and fog, but as time went by it seemed that recent memories grew sharper instead of diminishing, my life in the brothel parading past in shocking cinematic images in which I viewed myself as the leading character. And what I saw was so disgusting I could barely stand it.

"Airy, are you hungry?"

I looked up, trying to focus on Fehin, but his image seemed to shift and change, his face becoming one of those who frequented my room. The idea of food made me gag.

When he reached to help me up I moved away. I tried to form words but they wouldn't come. I finally shook my head, turning my face to the pillow. I heard him sigh and then the sound of his retreating footsteps. After that I heard the murmur of conversation as he spoke to the other man.

"She won't eat. What am I going to do?"

I heard the worry in his voice and felt tears form in my eyes for what he was going through. I was the reason for his concern, but I couldn't do anything about it.

"We have to get you two out of here," I heard the other man say in a low tone. "Once she's home you can find help."

Home made no sense to me. I had no home.

"We don't have the ring and Gunnar has not deigned to do anything for us."

"You don't know his reasons, Fehin. I've never known him to neglect something important like this. He must have his hands full fixing the time gaps. Do you realize how long she's been here? It's nearly six months now."

"You're probably right, but I can't stand to see her like this. I'm afraid she'll never come out of it."

"I think you should stake out Mr. Sand's house and make a plan to steal the ring."

I wanted to cry but no tears would come. I was empty and wanted to die. *Don't do it!* I shouted inside my head.

He appeared in the doorway. "Why shouldn't I do it, Airy?"

"It won't work," I managed to mumble.

He moved toward me, a smile on his face. "This is the first time I've heard you say anything in over a month. You're getting better."

I turned my back and closed my eyes.

CHAPTER TWENTY

FEHIN

I spent nearly every day in the alley next to Mr. Sand's house watching his comings and goings. So far no pattern had emerged. One morning he would leave at seven and get back at nine, the next day he wouldn't leave until eleven and be out until eight that night. I was beginning to think it was a waste of time until I realized that he was always out for at least an hour, and usually two. That gave me plenty of time to get inside and search. The problem was the maid. I hadn't seen her or him, but I figured a man like Mr. Sand would not want to do things for himself. What if she alerted the authorities?

This thing with Airy had left me oddly unsure of myself. And being without my magic made it worse. *Gunnar where in hell are you?* I called out in my mind. *Do you care at all about your charge, Airy? Well, if you do, she's sinking fast. If I don't get her out of here soon I'm sure she's going to die from starvation.* I wiped at the corners of my eyes. This was the first time I'd admitted how frightened I was. She was hardly eating, and I had the sense that she was consciously starving herself to death.

A moment later I heard the door close and watched Mr. Sand head down the stone steps to the street. He walked briskly away. As soon as he was out of sight I hurried up the steps. Magic or not I could still tell a convincing lie. I lifted the heavy lion-head knocker and let it fall.

"Yes?" the young woman asked, peering out at me from the crack in the door. "Mr. Sand is not here," she continued, ready to push the door closed. I placed my foot in the opening.

"Mr. Sand asked me to come," I began, thinking fast. "He wanted me to collect some papers he left in his study. My name is Silas Bret. Mr. Sand and I are on a board together." I smiled winningly.

When she hesitated I sent a telepathic message, hoping the gist of it would reach her. *This man is to be trusted.* I watched her face relax. Something must have gotten through because she pulled the door wide. "Come in, then," she invited.

I stood in the hall taking in her thin face, the tired look in her eyes. Blonde hair hung lank around her shoulders, the apron she wore too big for her narrow frame. "Can you show me to the study?"

"Of course," she said, seeming to come back to herself. "Follow me."

"You can go back to your duties," I said once we'd reached the room. "It will only take me a few minutes. I'll let myself out." I stared into her pale eyes putting on my most trustworthy expression.

She nodded and backed away and I heard her footsteps retreating down the hall. I hurried to the large desk and began pulling drawers open, my fingers clumsy and shaking. I searched each one systematically but found no ring. Damn! What if he'd sold it? He easily could have since there was no way the magic would work for him. I looked around the large office, noticing another cabinet against the wall. But this one was locked. I felt sure the ring was inside and looked around for a tool to pick the lock. I was hard at work with a small silver letter opener when I heard Mr. Sands bellow from the front hall. "Ane? Where are you?"

I looked around wildly, trying to find a place to hide. I heard him talking to the maid and then his hurried footsteps coming down the hall. I slipped out of the room and ran in the opposite direction, opening the first door I came to. A closet. I hid myself behind mops and brooms and buckets and held my breath.

"He isn't here!" I heard Mr. Sand yell. "Did he leave?"

"I don't know, sir. He said he'd let himself out."

"You are never to let anyone in here without my permission!" he shouted. I heard a thwack as he hit her and then her cry of pain.

"I'm sorry, sir."

"You best be on your best behavior if you don't want me to turn you out on the plains. I should never have agreed to take you on."

She sniffed. "He seemed so sincere with his dark eyes and dark hair. He had such a nice smile."

"Dark eyes and hair? That sounds like Fehin. Thin?"

"Yes, sir."

"Goddammit! I should have known. He wants that ring and that means he's with Airy. I'm going to find them and put them on the next boat that leaves for China. I'll be paid handsomely for an exotic pair." He let out a nasty laugh. "Go back to work. I have plans to make."

I heard him move away, the quiet sobs of the maid continuing as she followed him. Was the ring here or not?

I waited until I was sure Mr. Sand had left the house before I ventured out of the closet. In the downstairs hall close to the front door I ran into the maid, her eyes going wide when she saw me. "I thought you had gone," she said, looking around wildly. "If he catches you here he'll beat me."

"I'm leaving now and if you're smart you'll find another job. Mr. Sand is an evil bastard."

"There is no job for me. I'm lucky to have this one after—" She looked down.

"After what?"

"He took me off the street. If he hadn't I'd be dead by now."

"You mean you would have been hunted?"

She nodded. "I had no means, and my family had already been released into the wild."

"So there is no organization who will help find you a job or a place to stay?"

"No. I was lucky that Mr. Sand took me in."

I stared at her, wondering how she could explain this to me as though it was perfectly normal. "If I had that damn ring I'd take you out of here," I said.

"Ring? You mean the one with the pale stone? I know where it is."

"Where? I searched his office."

"He keeps it in the table next to his bed. I'll show you." She turned and gestured for me to follow.

Twenty minutes later I had the ring in my pocket and had convinced her to come with me, assuring her that the ring was magic and could take us to another time.

"Why don't you do it, then?" she asked as we left the house. "Take us out of here, I mean."

"My girlfriend is the only person it works for," I said. When I saw the expression that appeared on her face I realized she had hoped for more. "I'm sorry, Ane. I should have said."

"That's okay."

But it wasn't, and I felt bad for leading her on.

Jem was not happy when he saw Ane, his eyes narrowing in anger. "This is not a rescue mission," he hissed. "Every time you come and go it makes me more vulnerable to the nosy ones who would like to see me locked up. And bringing a woman here is especially suspicious."

"She needed to get away from Mr. Sand."

"Everyone here needs to get away from someone or something. Did you at least get the ring?"

I pulled it out of my pocket and held it out. "I did."

He gestured with his head toward Airy's room. "Good luck getting her to use it. That woman is seriously traumatized."

Ane moved to the doorway, staring in at Airy who lay on the bed with her back to us. "Is this your girlfriend?"

"She was before Mr. Sand sold her to the brothel. She hasn't come out of it yet."

Ane stared at me. "I knew several women who died working there."

"The doctor helped me get Airy out—the place has been closed down now."

"I heard from a friend that when the women don't do as they're told they send them to this room in the basement. It doesn't sound all that bad to me."

I looked at Jem. "Have you heard about this?"

He nodded. "It's solitary confinement, Fehin. Some can take it and others can't. And it also depends on how long they're left there. I wonder if that's what wrong with Airy. Just being a prostitute doesn't normally put you into a psychotic state."

"It could for someone like her. She's innocent and has a light- hearted spirit, always looking on the good side of everything. She takes the bad part of life to heart and wants to make it better." I glanced at her. "She's been severely damaged."

Jem shook his head and pressed his lips together. "I suggest you try and rouse her and get her to use the stone before she slips even further into the dark place she's gone."

I'd tried several times in the past week to rouse Airy enough to make her understand what she needed to do. Ane came and went, bringing back supplies with the money Jem gave her. I was attempting again to wake Airy from her stupor when I heard a crash against the door and then the sound of the locks giving way as it caved inward. Several men wearing uniforms and carrying battering rams stood in the doorway with Mr. Sand. Behind them were the police who rushed into the house and grabbed Ane and Jem before I could do anything to stop them. When I met Ane's unworried expression I realized immediately that she'd notified Mr. Sand of our whereabouts. "Why?" I asked.

"You have a girlfriend—there is nothing here for me."

The police grabbed me and tied my hands while Mr. Sand searched for Airy. A few minutes later he appeared carrying her. He smiled at me. "She's a bit worse for wear but I'll still get my money's worth," he said, heading out the door.

After I was dragged outside I turned my head to Jem who was cuffed and waiting to be put into a vehicle. "I'm sorry," I called.

"I knew it would finally come to this," he said, his eyes dark. A moment later he was shoved inside the cart.

Mr. Sand led the way to another cart driven by a Chinese man, depositing a limp Airy on the seat. The cop holding me pushed me inside and closed it up. "Take them to the holding pens," I heard Mr. Sand tell the driver. "I'll meet you there."

"Airy," I whispered, shaking her. But there was no response, her eyes closed.

By the time Mr. Sand reached the docks Airy and I had been placed in a cage with several others. She was barely awake, her head lolling against my shoulder. Mr. Sand came toward us with another Chinese man who looked to be a business owner. "The boy is fit and the girl will be once she's fattened up a bit. They would make an exotic pair of servants for someone wealthy."

The man looked us over, reaching through the bars to pinch Airy and try and rouse her. But she barely responded. "What has happened to this one?" he demanded, staring at Mr. Sand.

"She hasn't been fed properly. She may have been traumatized at the brothel, but she'll be recovered by the time you reach Shanghai."

He shook his head. "The price you named is too much. I'll give you half."

Mr. Sand looked taken aback. "Half? That's ridiculous. These two are very unusual--look at this red hair! Perhaps you can use them to make more slaves, ones that you can sell for a higher price."

"That requires years in which I will have no return on my investment. Half," he said again, his implacable gaze on Mr. Sand. He crossed his arms over his narrow chest.

There was a long moment in which I wondered what our destiny would be, but then Mr. Sand nodded. Money was exchanged and then Mr. Sand left us there without a backward glance.

An hour later we had been stripped and dressed in loose cotton tunics. The ring in my pocket was gone along with our clothing. We were led up the gangplank with the others in our same plight, and taken to the hold of the ship. The smells of excrement and coal mixed with the whiff of fear wafted toward us on a breeze that stopped as soon as they closed us in. It was hot and humid, and sweat beaded on my scalp, dripping down the sides of my face.

There was barely room to sit, the cage filled to capacity. I held Airy upright, her body swaying against me. Some were crying, others stood stoical, while others cast about for some way to get free. When I looked at Airy her eyes were open but I knew she didn't register where we were or what was going on. Maybe that was a blessing.

The trip was endless, the rocking of the ship immediately casting Airy into paroxysms of illness, her retching going on and on. Finally the guards took her away, tired of cleaning up after her. They did not bring her back. The rest of us had a bucket in which to do our business and just enough room to sit. The food they gave us consisted of either a gruel-like substance or bread and soured milk, our days filled with the creaks and groans of the ship and the sound of men hauling ropes and calling to each other in Chinese. The stench in the hold grew stronger with no air circulation, the heat a heavy weight that never lifted.

About three days into the trip a storm hit, our wire cage rocking back and forth until it finally tipped over, all of us falling into a tangle of sweaty legs and arms, the bucket's contents splashing across us. When we were righted again the guards did nothing to clean us up despite our shouting. Several had fevers and intestinal distress, but they were left to deal with it. I called out every chance I got, but the only response was a cattle prod that sent a buzz of electricity soaring through my body, leaving me weak and sick for several hours. When two of our group finally succumbed to the dysentery they were dragged from the cage and thrown overboard.

And then the bugs arrived. I figured they were drawn to us by the stench of our sweat and the excrement that had formed a crust on our tunics and skin. They flew into our eyes and bit us mercilessly, raising welts that itched and burned. We couldn't get away from them. We called to the guards for bug spray, for salves to stop the endless itching, but they only laughed, watching us like we were some novelty show. I wondered how they could treat merchandise this way, coming to the conclusion that they were not the owners and therefore didn't care.

I scanned into the darkness hoping to spot Airy, but I didn't see her anywhere. What had they done with her? I began to worry that she'd died and been thrown overboard, my panic growing as the days went by. The bugs remained. All of us were screaming now, our bodies bleeding where we'd scratched so hard we'd bitten into our skin. The flimsy tunics afforded no barrier as they found their way under them to sting and bite in places we couldn't reach. When the guards came to bring us food they only laughed, handing us our bowls of gruel before beating a hasty retreat as the swarms of gnats and mosquitoes discovered them.

We docked at some late hour, all of us so relieved that we cried soundlessly so as not to attract attention. Somehow we'd bonded in the days together, despite our lack of real conversation. Blessedly it was raining the next morning when we were led off the ship and down to a waiting cart. I reveled in the feeling of it on my skin, washing at least some of the filth from the disgusting tunic and my face and arms.

The dock was filled with the smell of horse dung and food, the cacophony of different languages, different colors of clothing, and shouting, a shock after the days in the dark. Boxes and barrels were stacked everywhere, men wearing raingear unloading them and calling out to each other. I opened my mouth to the rain before scanning for some glimpse of Airy. Even with the rain there was a brownish haze in the air that smelled of pollution.

When I finally saw her I let out a cry that was immediately silenced by a blow to the side of my head. *Airy!,* I called out telepathically, but she didn't turn from where she was being led to a heavy cart pulled by two horses. Her body was even thinner than I remembered, her eyes sunken in her head. A moment later a man grabbed me out of the cage.

"You come," he said, pulling me to the cart where Airy stood staring into space, her wet hair in tangles around a chalk-white face.

"Airy," I said in her ear as the driver urged the horses forward. I took hold of her arm but she didn't turn. I slapped her face and still she didn't turn. "What did they do to you?" I whispered. I finally gave up and examined our surroundings.

Enormous buildings stood abandoned in the shadows, smaller wooden ones built along side them. Roadways that had once been pavement had turned to sand and rock, with deep potholes filled with mud and horse dung. I saw no cars, heard nothing that had an engine. In the far distance through the rain and haze I saw skyscrapers, but from what I could tell they were no longer used, some of the spires broken and twisted. The economy seemed diminished and archaic compared with what I'd read of twenty-first century Shanghai, and I wondered if there'd been a nuclear war. If so I hoped the radiation was gone by now.

When Airy suddenly crumpled to the floor I cried out to the driver to stop, but he ignored me. I shouted as we navigated a street filled with people of every color, wares being hawked by the side of the road and hundreds of rustic houses that teetered up three stories or more, made of wood and thatch. The road narrowed and twisted, the sounds of the harbor fading behind us. But now the faces I saw were ravaged, the people as thin as scarecrows, tattered clothing hanging off their thin frames. The air of despondency grew as we moved along narrowing streets, working our way into the muddle of what seemed to be the center of town. Had all human decency been swallowed by the maw of commerce? Where were the people who cared?

I was on my knees next to Airy feeling for a pulse when we came to an abrupt halt in front of an imposing building of brick. The driver unlocked the gate that held us in and grabbed my arm. "She's dead," I told him, tears flowing down my face.

He leaned down and felt her neck before picking her up. "She not dead," he said. "Come," he ordered, pulling me by my chain. As if I had a choice.

A plain looking Chinese woman dressed in a simple linen tunic opened the heavy door. "What is wrong with woman?"

"She's very sick," I answered. "She needs acupuncture and herbs and good food."

The woman pursed her lips and shook her head. "No acupuncture or herbs for your kind. Must have money to pay."

"What about food? This woman is worth something to you, isn't she? She'll die if you don't help her."

She shrugged, gesturing to the man who carried Airy to follow her down a hall. She pointed to a room and said something in Chinese. The man went ahead of me and placed Airy on a mattress on the floor. It was the only thing in the square windowless room. She left us there and closed and locked the door.

I sat next to Airy and pulled her head into my lap. Her tunic was not nearly as dirty as mine was, her hair cleaner as well. What had she gone through on the boat? I didn't want to think about it, especially because of how close to death she seemed.

The horror of what our lives had become rolled over me, bringing with it a seething black anger. Why hadn't Gunnar come for us? Why hadn't Airy's light beings helped? What had we done to deserve this fate? I had never felt so helpless as I stared down at Airy. Her skin held a death-like pallor, her normally rosy lips bloodless and pale. I realized I was crying when I noticed the tears landing on her face. I placed a kiss on her forehead wishing I could turn back the clock. What could I possibly do to save her?

CHAPTER TWENTY ONE
AIRY

arkness fills my chest. I am overcome with it. I barely remember who I was or how I got here, but I do remember the life I've been leading and the terrible things I've done. I see the man I used to love, but I have no feelings, my heart as cold as a stone. He's attempting to talk with me but I can never allow him to know what I've become. Let him remember some fantasy of me—let him think I'm the Airy he once knew. I have no name for this, no name for who I am now. It is too dark to name and I am down too deep to find my way back. What has been done to me has seared into my soul. There is no return. The boat. I let out a scream, the recent memory so clear, the reality washing over me like a tsunami, everything that came before swallowed up in that wave, leaving me blessedly empty.

"Airy? Airy!"

I see him frowning over me but I can't speak, my throat as dry as parchment. I hear him sob, a tear falling on my skin and burning into me. I want to reassure him. I'm not dead. Not yet. The realization arrives like a bright light. No more pain, no more fear.

"Help!" *I hear him shout.* 'Something's wrong with Airy, she's…"

By the time the door opens I'm floating on a sea of calm, water drifting over me as I sink lower and lower, letting the darkness take me into the depths.

CHAPTER TWENTY TWO
FEHIN

When I grabbed Airy around the middle and pulled her up to sitting, her body slumped against my arms. And when I lowered my ear to listen I couldn't hear any breath coming from her mouth. "Someone help!"

The door opened and the woman appeared, a frown on her features. She came over to the bed and took Airy's hand, listening with her fingers on her wrist. She shook her head, her eyes meeting mine. "Tomorrow we burn her," she said, backing out. "Renegotiate price."

"Dead? No—NO!!!!!!" I began CPR, tears pouring down my cheeks and onto her face as I pinched her nose closed and breathed into her slack mouth.

I did this for a long time before I finally sat back on my heels. "I love you, you love me—there's no life without you!" My voice cracked and I had to stop, my gaze on the still form on the bed. She was so thin, so pale. This couldn't be happening. I let out a scream and fell forward, my head next to hers. "No! No!!! No!!!"

The door opened and a heavy-set man came in. "You want we take body?" he asked.

"No, please leave her with me until morning," I begged through my tears.

"Then you be quiet," he commanded.

I sat there thinking about miracles, hoping that somehow either Gunnar would appear, or the beings of light Airy had told me about. They could bring her back to life. But as the hours ticked by I realized this was it. Airy was truly gone.

I spent the night on the hard mattress, holding her in my arms. I knew this was deranged and probably ghoulish behavior, but I couldn't let her go. Not yet. I kept waking, thinking it was all a bad dream, expecting her to be looking at me with that bright expression I knew so well, the one before she made some sarcastic remark and fell to laughing. I felt every rib as I shifted her in my arms, her head lolling back to reveal sharp cheekbones beneath sunken closed eyes. My tears continued, as though crying might release her from whatever magic spell had taken her away.

It was late in the night when I began wishing we were home in Milltown, my mind turning to our time there. "Why did we ever do this, Airy?" I asked the cold and stiffening body in my arms. "Why did we think that traveling through time would be fun? I want to be back in Milltown before it all happened. I want you back." Tears tracked down my face and dripped onto her grayish skin. "Please, someone help us!" I begged, looking up at the ceiling, as thought the light beings would suddenly gather us both up and take us away.

An overwhelming pain moved through my belly as I looked down on her in my arms. I held her close, sobbing and trying to be quiet in case the big man came back and took her away. I couldn't let her go. I had a vision of the fire where her body would burn, turning her into ash. I let out a shriek so loud I knew one of them would come any second and grab her away from me. A moment later I was spinning, darkness sucking me into its embrace as the two of us whirled away.

I landed in the woods behind the college, close to the spot we'd left from. Airy was as dead as she had been, rigor mortis setting in. It was afternoon, and as I scanned around I saw our earlier selves standing fifty feet away talking. "Don't do it!" I shouted when I saw Airy rub the ring. They both turned, staring at me holding Airy in my arms. A second later we began to fade. Airy had become transparent. Two sets of us could not exist in the same timeline. And then we were gone.

CHAPTER TWENTY THREE
AIRY

"Did you see that?" I asked, grabbing Fehin's arm.

He gave me a look that said he did, but the frown on his face and the faraway expression seemed to indicate something more.

"How can we be standing here and see ourselves just over there? I looked dead."

"We must have already done this trip and run into trouble. You know two sets of us can't exist in the same timeline."

"Run into trouble? Is that what you call it? I'd say it was more than trouble, Fehin." I stared at him, trying to decipher the weird expression on his face. "What do you know that I don't?"

His eyes filled and he pulled me into his arms. "I know that I love you and I don't want to risk losing you," he whispered huskily.

I pulled away. "Just because it looked like I was dead doesn't mean I will be. Are you going to tell me what's going on? Because I would really like to use the stone now."

Fehin grabbed the moonstone ring out of my hand and threw it high into the air. I watched it split apart into a million tiny crystals before evaporating into nothingness. "Why did you do that?" I shouted. "That ring was given to me by my mother and belonged to my grandmother!" I glared at him, but he didn't meet my gaze, his focus on something in the far distance. I grabbed his upper arm. "And now I can't take us anywhere! Are you going to tell me what's—"

My sentence was interrupted by Fehin's sudden need to kiss me, his mouth finding mine before I could protest. I melted into him, moved by his passion. When he pulled away he kept hold of me, as though I might disappear like my ring.

"Are you going to explain why you just destroyed my ring? And why did it break apart like that?"

"Airy, what I said is true. We already took this trip and it ended in disaster. Didn't you get the feeling when you saw me carrying your limp body, that maybe we were being warned?"

"Well, yes. I did think it was kind of weird, but I don't remember anything. Do you?"

His lips pressed together. "I'm afraid I do."

"What happened to us? And why can't I remember?"

He shook his head. "I can't tell you, Airy. It's too terrible. As to why you can't remember and I can, I have no idea."

I grabbed his arm, twisting him to look at me. "You better tell me or I'll—"

His dark eyes met mine. "You'll what? The ring is gone now and the chance of traveling through time is gone with it."

"And a good thing too," Gunnar said, appearing out of nowhere.

I gasped and stumbled backward. "Why are *you* here?" I asked, watching him push his hands through his tangled gray hair. He looked more tired than I'd ever seen him.

The druid stared at Fehin. "You know, don't you?"

Fehin looked startled for a moment, and then he smiled, glancing at me. He nodded.

"Know what? Why won't anyone tell me what's going on?"

Fehin's gaze met mine. "I'm like Gunnar. I'm a time lord."

I shook my head frowning. "A time lord—since when is Gunnar a time lord? Last I heard he traveled through time, but—"

"I've always been a time-lord, Airy. But there was no need to broadcast it. I only told Fehin because of his questions when he was lost in the in between place."

"What in between place? Okay, you two. Someone better explain what's going on here."

Fehin took hold of my hand, twining his fingers through mine. "I wasn't sure how I managed to move us back here to warn our other selves. I figured it was love that did it. But now it all makes sense."

"So you remember everything and I have no memory at all?"

"You never went anywhere, so how could you remember it?"

"You didn't either, Fehin, so how come you—oh, I get it. You remember because you're now a time lord? This news has got to swell your head even more." I let out an exasperated sigh.

"Why didn't you save us?" Fehin asked Gunnar, ignoring me.

"I was too busy trying to repair the gaps in time and getting things into balance. Too much time went by while you were—" he glanced at Airy.

"In Mr. Sand's world?" Fehin supplied, his eyes going dark.

I watched the two of them, irritated that I was left completely out of the conversation. "I hope one of you fills me in soon," I grumbled.

"Believe me, Airy, you don't want to know," Fehin said, looping an arm around my shoulders.

I pulled away. "You don't get off that easily, either one of you. If we aren't going to make the trip I want to know what happened."

He watched me for a moment before turning to Gunnar again. "What about the tribe, Gunnar? Are they still in the past or--?"

Gunnar shook his head. "You prevented it from happening."

"Can I go back and make it right for Spotted Elk? If I don't, he—"

"I know," Gunnar interrupted, staring at me. "Let me think on it."

"If I'm a time-lord now, when will I meet the other time-lords? And who decides these things?"

"Messing about with history is never a good idea, Fehin. As I said before, moving a tribe back one hundred years changes the entire trajectory of births and deaths. I think leaving them where they are is best."

I gasped, listening. "Are you saying we moved an entire tribe of Native Americans? Were they famous?"

"Spotted Elk was one of them," Fehin mumbled. He looked up at Gunnar again. "He said he saw it in a vision. He was so happy."

Gunnar frowned. "This kind of thing is against the rules. And from what I heard he only had the vision about two travelers from the future, not traveling one hundred years into the past."

"So you were there."

"Not there, exactly. I'm tasked with making sure things like this don't happen."

"And yet you let us do it," Fehin answered.

Gunnar didn't reply, his gaze slanting to me before he stared at his feet.

I moved away from them and sat on the ground with my back to a tree. These two annoying *men* had dashed my hopes of traveling into the past. Fehin was now a time lord? Good gods, I'd never hear the end of it. And the only thing I was good at was talking to trees and my ring, which I now didn't have. Despite him saying I didn't want to know what happened, I did. And I had a right to know. Tears pricked my eyes as I listened to Fehin and Gunnar discussing 'matters of grand importance'. But every time I glanced up Gunnar was staring at me. What was with the significant looks?

The tree had a soothing effect, but I needed to talk with someone—a human friend. My mother was out after the argument we had just a few hours ago. And Fehin, my usual confidant, was out now due to his 'new and improved' status. The only person I could think of was Carla. I was just about to get up and head toward her apartment when I felt the familiar pull of the ether and spun away into darkness.

CHAPTER TWENTY FOUR
FEHIN

I looked toward the tree where Airy had been sitting just a moment before. "Where's Airy?"

"You haven't figured it out yet, have you?"

"Figured what out?"

Gunnar smirked. "It's not you, Fehin. It's Airy. She's the time lord."

"What? Why didn't you say?"

"I decided to let things unfold. Far be it for me to interfere."

"She was pissed at me, Gunnar."

The druid grinned. "Well, she won't be now."

"So if I'm not a time-lord how did I get us back here in time to warn our former selves?"

"It wasn't you who did it."

"But Airy was dead in my arms—how could she--?"

"Her former self brought her back."

"But how is that possible if she doesn't remember?"

"Time lords are different, Fehin. They have access to all time in all dimensions."

I shook my head, shielding my eyes from the late afternoon sunlight slanting through the branches. "And the ring? It broke apart when I threw it. And how come I remember everything that happened to us?"

"The ring was no longer needed. As to why you remember—I suppose it's because you're a wizard. Now why don't you contact her telepathically and find out where she went."

CHAPTER TWENTY FIVE
AIRY

"How did I get here?" I asked, staring at Carla sitting at her kitchen table.

She laughed. "You have a ring, one that takes you through time? Or don't you remember that?"

I held up my hand showing her my empty finger. "Ring is gone, Carla—Fehin threw it into the air and it disintegrated into a million pieces."

Her eyes widened. "Really. Hmm…what were you doing right before you ended up here?"

I pulled out a chair and sat next to her. "Fehin and Gunnar were discussing Fehin's new status as time lord and…I was sitting with my back against a tree and wishing I had someone to talk to since I felt so crummy and left out…and I thought of you and wished I could sit here and have a cup of tea and get your take on things."

Carla rose. "Well, if that's what you want let's get to it," she said, moving to click on the electric teakettle. She turned, leaning against the counter. "So, you got here without your ring. That's interesting, don't you think?"

I stared at her, noticing the smile hovering around her mouth. "Yes it is. Maybe Fehin heard my thoughts and sent me here."

"Is that part of what a time lord does—sends people into the ether?"

"I know nothing about time lords."

There was a knock on the door and then it opened, revealing Fehin and Gunnar. "There you are," Fehin said, hurrying toward me as though he couldn't stand the idea of me being out of his sight.

I gazed at Gunnar. "Do you have an answer for how I got myself here without my ring?"

He grinned, his normally dour expression completely changing in that one simple act. "Can you guess?"

Fehin grabbed my hand and I heard the words in my head, *it's you, not me*. When I looked at him he was smiling.

"I'm the time lord?"

"You're the time lord," Gunnar parroted back.

I opened my mouth and closed it, trying to wrap my mind around this turn of events. "But how? Why?"

"There is no real reason why, Airy. As to how, the time lord council has decreed it."

Fehin twined his fingers through mine. "It makes sense after everything that happened. Once you remember everything will come clear."

But I barely heard him.

EPILOGUE

It took months before Airy's memories began to surface. Her horror grew with each one, tears coming nearly every day. I comforted her and tried to be gentle as I filled in the missing blanks. But it was difficult and I worried about her state of mind disintegrating as she revisited that bleak time.

We moved back in with Carla, who loved us being there, and was interested in everything I revealed about the dark days in Milltown.

"Sabre toothed tigers?" she gasped.

Airy stared at me, her expression changing as the memory came back. "And woolly rhinos and Neanderthals."

"I hate to say this, but I wish I'd seen them," Carla said, laughing.

A few days later Carla handed me my bead necklace. "Found these on your dresser and decided they needed to be restrung."

I didn't question how they'd gotten from wherever we'd been to this Milltown as I took them and hooked the necklace around my neck. "Thanks, Carla. These came from the Sioux we relocated. Spotted Elk gave them to me."

"Spotted Elk," she whispered reverently. "You did have some incredible adventures."

With the trauma I still felt about Airy's decline and subsequent death, I had a need to be close to her to assure myself that she was really here and alive. It didn't seem to irritate her that I followed her around like a puppy, afraid to let her out of my sight. And at night I held her close, worried at first to even try and kiss her once the memory of her time in the brothel began to surface.

"I won't initiate anything until you're ready," I promised every night before we exchanged the one chaste goodnight kiss. I hoped for both of our sakes that she wouldn't enter that terrible dark place she'd been in.

It was several months before she let me know she was ready, kissing me in a way that indicated what she wanted. Tears were on her cheeks the first few times she let me touch her. "Are you sure, Airy--would you rather talk?"

But she shook her head, as though she had to get through this in order to heal. And when she did want to talk, sharing some horrible experience that had appeared in her mind, we both ended up crying, holding each other close until the images faded and she could realize where she was.

When I asked about the memories she said, "I remember the events but I don't remember how it affected me. It's like I'm watching a movie about someone I care about."

I thought of the light beings, wondering if they'd spared Airy the true terror and shock of what she'd experienced. Her death and what led up to it remained a secret, something she never recalled. And I was thankful for it.

It was months before I felt we turned a corner, the old Airy appearing again, laughing and teasing me as we celebrated what we felt for each other. Her spirit was as it had always been—light and airy just like her name.

It was six months later when she began to talk about Spotted Elk and the tribe. "I think we need to do that part of our trip again," she said, staring at me pointedly.

"Gunnar said no," I reminded her.

"I'm a time lord now, so there will be no rips or gaps in time, and no mistakes."

"Really, Airy? How can you be so sure?"

She smiled a secret smile.

If you liked this book please leave a review on Amazon!
https://www.amazon.com/Nikki-Broadwell/e/B007EE1LN0
Just click on the cover and scroll down to review!! One or two
lines are sufficient.

Visit my website, www.nikkibroadwell.com for more
information on me, my books, deals and promos, and snippets
of useless information. Thanks for reading!

www.ingramcontent.com/pod-product-compliance
Lightning Source LLC
Chambersburg PA
CBHW020108180626
46812CB00006B/2523

* 9 7 8 0 9 9 7 9 9 4 1 4 8 *